A Candlelight
Ecstasy Romance ®

SALLY RACED THROUGH THE RAIN TO HER CAR. P.J. SLID IN BESIDE HER. . . .

They were both drenched. He took one look at her and began to laugh. "There was a girl, who had a curl . . ."

Sally heard herself answering, "And when she was good . . ."

But before she could finish, his mouth covered hers. "She was marvelous," he murmured.

She leaned back, mischief shining in her eyes. ". . . and when she was bad . . . she was better!"

Pete's eyes flew wide in surprise. Sally clapped a hand over her mouth. "I didn't mean to say that! Don't get any ideas."

"Too late, Sally soufflé. I've already got 'em."

"Decker, what are you? A magician? A snake charmer? I had every intention of being angry with you. Telling my father *you'd* help me get my job back!"

Pete's low laugh whipped up her desire. "I'm both, my sweet." He slanted a sexy look in her direction. "And now let's head home while I've still got you under my spell."

A CANDLELIGHT ECSTASY ROMANCE ®

DOUBLE PLAY

Natalie Stone

Published by
Dell Publishing Co., Inc.
1 Dag Hammarskjold Plaza
New York, New York 10017

A CANDLELIGHT ECSTASY ROMANCE®

Published by
Dell Publishing Co., Inc.
1 Dag Hammarskjold Plaza
New York, New York 10017

To Mort and Mil, who believed in us from the start. Our love and thanks.

Copyright © 1983 by Sally Goldenbaum and Adrienne Staff

All rights reserved. No part of this book may be reproduced or transmitted in any form or by any means, electronic or mechanical, including photocopying, recording or by any information storage and retrieval system, without the written permission of the Publisher, except where permitted by law.

Dell ® TM 681510, Dell Publishing Co., Inc.

Candlelight Ecstasy Romance®, 1,203,540, is a registered trademark of Dell Publishing Co., Inc., New York, New York.

ISBN: 0-440-12119-1

Printed in the United States of America
First printing—December 1983

To Our Readers:

We have been delighted with your enthusiastic response to Candlelight Ecstasy Romances®, and we thank you for the interest you have shown in this exciting series.

In the upcoming months we will continue to present the distinctive sensuous love stories you have come to expect only from Ecstasy. We look forward to bringing you many more books from your favorite authors and also the very finest work from new authors of contemporary romantic fiction.

As always, we are striving to present the unique, absorbing love stories that you enjoy most—books that are more than ordinary romance.

Your suggestions and comments are always welcome. Please write to us at the address below.

Sincerely,

The Editors
Candlelight Romances
1 Dag Hammarskjold Plaza
New York, New York 10017

CHAPTER ONE

"All right, folks, now watch the screen closely!" The voice booming off the walls in the small screening room belonged to cameraman Bruce Warren, affectionately called "Beaver" by his colleagues at WQEK-TV. "I call this little vignette 'Sally's Farewell.' "

"Oh, Beaver . . . no, not on my first day back!" Sally Denning groaned as she slipped into a chair next to her redheaded production assistant, Robin Gifford.

"Shhh," Robin hushed her to silence. "This sounds good."

The small audience watched expectantly as the lights dimmed and Sally's familiar figure appeared on the small screen. Standing inside an open doorway, she was carefully scrutinizing the bustle taking place in the background. She was a striking woman, slender, tanned, with a noticeable sparkle in her deep hazel eyes. A small pad of paper and pencil in one hand, she was watching, unnoticed in the frantic confusion. Behind her, muscular, bare-torsoed men moved back and forth, throwing towels in smelly heaps on the tile floor, slamming metal locker doors, shouting to one another over the rush of steaming showers. Their tanned bodies glistened with sweat across the bulging muscles as they toweled themselves and made their way about the crowded room, littered now with bats, helmets, and discarded baseball uniforms.

As WQEK's newest sportscaster, Sally was diligently covering the Kansas City Royals' spring training in Florida and preparing her viewers back home in Lawrence for the upcoming baseball season.

At that moment two uniformed men, their faces grim, came into focus on the screen and walked toward Sally. She stiffened visibly as they approached.

"Lady . . ." the first began, his voice all but drowned out by the background noises.

Sally's brows drew together. She threw the towering guard a challenging look and shouted over the din. "It's all right, I'm press!" She drew herself up to her full five feet five inches and defiantly displayed the official button attached to her thin summer blouse. Her eyes were intense, glaring.

"I'm sorry, miss, but you're still a dame, and you'll soon be more than 'pressed' if we let you stay in this wild den!" The ruddy-faced guard laughed at his own bumbling attempt at humor, then continued, "Lady, we got our orders, ya know."

The look on the fledgling broadcaster's face was clear. She was not daunted by their uniformed authority or by their brawn. She stood firm and resolute, turned away from the guards, and began jotting notes on her white pad. The two men exchanged glances. Then, as the camera faithfully recorded every movement, they smoothly took hold of her elbows, lifted her off the ground with a practiced swoop, carried her through the door, deposited her like a sack of feathers in a colorless hallway, and slammed the heavy metal door behind them.

Low chuckles broke out in the editing room as the screen whitened. Sally threw back her head and laughed,

10

a honey-coated sound that was instantly infectious. "What Beaver is not revealing to you, Jim and Robin, is that *he* was thrown out too! Aiding and abetting the enemy, I think. Although"—she threw him an accusing grin— "you really weren't much help!"

"My job is to film, Sal," he teased. "Actually though, if you thought that locker room was hard to crack, you should have been with me the day I tried to film P. J. Decker's boudoir."

"Beaver!"

The bearded cameraman grinned mischievously. "Well, not bedroom exactly, although the scuttlebutt had it that that's where he did most of his off-field entertaining. In truth, I merely wanted a glimpse of the superstar's Florida apartment before you did that interview."

"Oh, Sally, an interview with P. J. Decker!" Robin piped up as the lights came on. "Fantastic! But how did you stand it, being that close to Kansas City's most fantastic muscles? What I wouldn't give to watch *him* ripple and stretch!"

"Oh, Robin! You had better go cold turkey on those romance novels you keep stashed in your top drawer." Her hazel eyes sparkled in amusement. "Actually, I never even got that interview."

"What rotten luck!" Robin said forlornly.

"You're right," Sally answered. "For both of us!"

Beaver answered the question in Robin's eyes by flicking off the lights and turning to the text tape.

Sally braced herself, knowing what was coming— knowing the flood of emotions that would wash over her. It was still so vivid in her mind. The screen filled with flickering images, but Sally closed her eyes. She didn't need a videotape to take her back to that warm Florida day. Each moment was still imprinted in her memory in vivid technicolor. She had been standing inside the fence, back behind third base. She was a yard or two away from the cameras, avoiding their heat and trying desperately to catch a faint wisp of breeze in the still afternoon sun. Notebook in hand, she watched the changing patterns of men and light across the emerald field. The sun was hot on her shoulders, hot on her face and chest. Her white cotton sundress clung to her and she absentmindedly unbuttoned the top button, loosening the material across her breasts. She fanned her face and neck with the open edge of the notebook, but her eyes never left the field.

There was a man on first and another was up at bat. The pitcher wound up, delivered, and the umpire's signal flashed—strike! Oh, oh, Sally worried, nibbling at the end of her pencil. Bottom of the third, two outs, score tied. Come on fellas. "Come on Rao!" she yelled, her voice ringing through the nearly empty stadium. The catcher tapped the plate with his bat, took his position, and locked his eye back on the ball. "Strike two!" Sally crossed her fingers and held her breath. The third pitch was thrown, hit, and the batter slipped into first a narrow second before the ball.

"That's the way, Rao. Good hit!" She flashed the okay sign. Rao grinned and tugged playfully at the bill of his cap from across the field.

From under the weight of his camera, sprouting from his shoulder like some strange appendage, Beaver grinned at her. He was her chief cameraman and he and his crew had been working with the lights and sound equipment all afternoon in preparation for the scheduled interview with the Royals' coach at the end of this exhibition game. Sally grinned back, sharing both his tiredness and his enjoyment. What a glorious day. Kansas City and Lawrence were just beginning to shed their winter coats when she left, but here in Florida it was summer, warm and sultry, redolent with blooms. Between games, scheduled interviews, and the obligatory press parties, Sally had found time to immerse herself in the sun, the scent of fresh flowers, the taste of fresh fish and ripe fruit. The result was a gorgeous tan and a body sleek and svelte as any athlete's. She smiled to herself and leaned back against the fence, looking out at the field. The next batter was on his way from the dugout. And talk about looking good! It was P. J. Decker, the Royals' glamour boy third baseman. The sunlight glinted off his uniform, outlining every muscle revealed by the tight stretch of the material. He was fairly tall for a ball player, lean and hard, with a flat stomach and slim hips. A little lanky, perhaps, for Sally's taste, but there was no denying his sex appeal—even if it hadn't been broadcasted from the sports page more often than not. There was no mistaking his presence. He wore his sensuality like a second skin. It was there, undeniable. Decker stood at the plate, the bat swinging loosely between his hands.

On the mound the pitcher had a somewhat harried look on his face. Decker faced him, swung his bat twice in a circle over his head. The muscles rippled across his shoulders and chest, bunching and flowing as he rounded the swing. Then he planted his left foot, rested his bat on his shoulder, and thrust his head toward the pitcher.

Sally had watched him enough to know this was only a stall. Something was missing. Just as the pitcher nodded for a signal, Decker stepped out and away from the plate. He stretched, spreading his legs wide and bending from the waist, leaning first across one bulging thigh, then the other. The "flies," as the players' wives not too affectionately called the baseball groupies who hugged the fence, game after game, gave voice—wolf whistling, calling Decker's name, shouting a variety of interesting offers. Decker flicked his head in their direction, flashed them his famous wink, and strolled back to the plate.

Sally grimaced, then let it slide into a grin. What a showboat the man was! There was no denying it—Decker was one of a kind. Not to Sally's own taste, but definitely a crowd pleaser.

By now the poor pitcher was sweating. She could see the stains spreading slowly across the small of his back. He twisted his cap, wiped his brow, and signaled again. Again Decker resumed his stance and immediately Sally's practiced eye noted the difference. *This* was the practiced stance that had driven home twelve runs in the past week and a half, and fired the team's hopes for the division title. Now every muscle in his body was tense, every ounce of concentration leveled on the ball. She could read his fierceness in the narrowing of his eyes beneath his cap, the solid cut of his jaw, the stillness that enveloped him. Then the ball flew. There was the loud crack of contact and the ball reversed direction and hissed into left field. It was touched, dropped, picked up and thrown, but not before two men were home and Decker was safe on third.

Sally cheered, waving her straw hat over her head. "Way to go, Decker!" Decker glanced over his right shoulder and for a second they shared a grin of pure pleasure. Then his concentration hardened and all eyes turned to the next batter. It was Hernandez, the Royals' new powerhouse hitter, and Decker edged closer to home. A fast curve ball whizzed through the air, was hit hard, and sailed toward the left-field line. Decker shielded his eyes against the searing sunlight and stepped back. As everyone watched in dismay, he slipped at the very moment the ball whistled over third base. Dismay turned to frozen disbelief as the speeding ball crashed into the broad shoulder of the winner of the Most Valuable Player award.

Behind him, frozen in horror, Sally could see the bone-breaking impact of the ball. It spun Decker around, lifted him off his feet, and threw him back against the fence. As he hit the ground, Sally ran and reached him before his body stopped rolling. She braced his head gently as his body jerked convulsively, the pain spearing through him

14

in muscle-cramping agony. She ran her hand soothingly over his forehead. "Easy, P. J. It'll be all right." Then the coach was there, the team doctor on his heels, the umpire, manager, players. Decker lay in the middle of the circle, his eyes clenched tight, the tears of pain oozing beneath his lashes. His face was white and drawn with pain. His eyes flickered open for a moment and he managed a grin as his eyes met hers. "My very own angel of mercy. I must have died and gone to heaven."

As the doctor touched the injured shoulder, P. J. swallowed a moan. Sally wrapped her fingers around his hand and felt the crushing pressure of his grip. The coach pushed the crowd back and she started to move away, but P. J.'s hand held her fast. "Don't leave me, Florence Nightingale," he mumbled incoherently. Sally returned the pressure and stayed at his side. She held his hand as they lifted him on the stretcher, held on as the ambulance drove across the sun-drenched field to collect its burden. Held it still as the ambulance, siren screaming, raced for the hospital. It was only when the doctor administered the first of the anesthetic that P. J. released his hold on her. As the drug took effect and the pain eased, his fingers loosened and his eyes grew dim. "Be here." His voice was thick and husky. "I want a better look at what's attached to this hand I've been holding. Promise?"

Sally glanced uncomfortably around the room, then down into those questioning brown eyes. "Yes, P. J. Sure."

Beaver found her there in the waiting room hours later and brought her a cup of coffee. "Didn't expect you'd still be around."

Sally shrugged and gazed into the murky depths of her cup. "Anything to get an interview." She laughed shyly. Then her green and brown flecked eyes looked up into his and she spoke softly. "Actually, Beaver, I don't know what I'm doing here. This all feels like some part of a

15

crazy dream. What *am* I doing here? I gave up fan clubs in the seventh grade, and I don't think hero worship has ever been my style. I don't know." She sighed, impatient with her own uncharacteristic behavior. Following an injured stranger to the hospital was one thing, but being beguiled by the Royals' playboy of the year was quite another! Yet she found herself riveted to the chair by the memory of those brown eyes. Each time she convinced herself it was time to go, she'd feel them on her face and settle back on the hard vinyl chair.

Then the decision was taken from her hands. With a snap the recovery room doors swung open. "Out of the way, everyone," called the doctor. "Out of the way, please. Mr. Decker is fine. What he needs now is a little rest and quiet. And . . . what?" He bent over his patient who was speaking softly. Then the white-cloaked figure looked up and his eyes swept the room. He signaled to Sally. Puzzled, she stepped to the side of P. J.'s stretcher.

P. J. Decker raised one droopy lid and peered up at her. "Is that my Florence Nightingale?"

She grinned. "Welcome back."

His lips moved again and Sally leaned down to catch the words. But instead of speaking, he turned his face just at that moment, his timing perfect, and kissed her on the mouth.

"Just my way of saying thank you. It's all I can manage on a gurney."

"A handshake would have been more than sufficient," Sally sputtered, half angry, half laughing.

Decker was smiling as they wheeled him away. Sally frowned at Beaver to forestall any of his wise remarks, but beneath her cool facade she had to admit that the kiss had tasted good—very good indeed.

And it was that memory, hidden behind the guise of kindness, that prompted Sally's visit to the hospital the next day. During a lull in the filming, she grabbed a handful of daisies from a street vendor, hopped a cab, and spent the short ride anticipating Decker's reaction. Would he still be so weak she'd sit by his bed and hold his hand again? Interesting thought . . . The cab slid to a stop at the main entrance and Sally paid the driver. She asked the receptionist for P. J.'s room number and headed for the fifth floor. But P. J. Decker was harder to visit than the queen of England. First she had to get past the fish-eyed head nurse at the nurses' station. Then she found the entire end of the fifth floor blocked by a bevy of Florida beauties.

"Excuse me, I'd like to see Mr. Decker . . ." Sally approached the entourage with an air of authority. She had, after all, escorted him to the hospital.

"You'll have to wait your turn, sweetie. They only let three in at a time," drawled a braless blonde in a bright blue Royals' T-shirt.

"And they're taking pictures. Can you believe it? If I had just gotten here a half hour sooner, maybe I could be the one perched on the side of lover boy's bed!" chimed in her red-haired companion.

The blonde laughed. "That's one way of getting into bed with Decker!"

Sally looked from one to the other and shook her head. "That's show biz, I guess," she mumbled as she started to turn away.

"Aren't you going to wait, sweetie?"

Sally cast a glance back over her shoulder. "No. I have more important things to do. And it looks like Mr. Decker is *not* in need of additional cheer." With a toss of her tawny head, she walked quickly down the hallway.

An elderly man sat in a wheelchair near the elevator. With a soft smile Sally wished him well and placed the daisies in his lap.

"Flowers from a pretty lady. That's the nicest thing that's happened to me in a long time."

17

"Well, it couldn't have happened to a nicer fellow," Sally answered, savoring the sudden sparkle in his tired eyes. Then she rode the next car down.

"Sally . . . Sally? You with us?"

Sally opened her eyes with a jerk. The lights were on in the editing room and the end of the tape was flapping noisily against the projection table.

"Oh, Sally," Robin groaned. "It's even worse seeing it than reading about all the gory details in the sports pages the past weeks. Poor thing. Such a beautiful body!"

"And it looks like that beautiful body is going to be out of commission for some time. It sure put a damper on those last weeks of spring training."

"Well, if you can believe it," interjected Jim Stafford, Sally's cobroadcaster, "the accident seems to be causing waves right here. Even the station manager seems affected. Williams stormed through here this morning muttering something about Decker's disaster. Funny, but I never imagined him as much of a sports fan."

Sally furrowed her brow. "Hmmm . . . me neither. But I guess good baseball means good news and even busy station managers would be concerned, I guess." She brushed a lose strand of sun-bleached hair behind one ear. "But as for me, I've had enough of P. J. Decker for one day." Sally stood and stretched her tan, trim frame. "The team *still* looked good, with or without the bachelor of the year. I think once the rest of the team realizes Decker's presence doesn't guarantee miracles, that he isn't some kind of a god, they'll be just fine."

"Spoken like a true, unbiased sports reporter!" Jim said facetiously, slipping a friendly arm over her slender shoulders. "What's with you, Sally? You suddenly seem to have it in for this guy."

Sally paused and stared at the blank screen for a moment, then answered hesitantly. "Sorry, Jim, I don't know what's bugging me about him. Maybe it's the superstar status, the playboy role with all the hovering, adoring fans. I never did find that very appealing." Carefully she skirted her own confusion over the unsettling effect the mention of his name seemed to have had on her these past few days. Her eyes brightened as she added, "But I *do* admire his greatness as a ball player, Jim. Watching him play ball is a thrill. It's like watching a disciplined ballet dancer. I had a brother who once played ball that way . . . who had Decker's potential. Sometimes he reminds me of what Matt might have been." Her voice trailed off as she seemed momentarily lost in an old memory. Jim shifted from one foot to the other, feeling like an intruder, yet touched by this new insight into his attractive, talented coworker. "So . . ." Sally broke the awkward silence. "There's no need to worry, my friend." She patted the hand still resting on her shoulder. "I'll stick to his baseball expertise on the air. His personal life really isn't a factor here, I know, and I shall not make it one! We'll leave the sexy innuendoes for the tabloids!" She smiled brightly. "Come on now, let's bury ourselves in these notes for the weekend special on spring training. We'll get this season off to a terrific start!"

Sally edged her little two-seater convertible into the employee parking lot, found a space not far from the main entrance, and slipped a pass under the windshield wiper. She'd have to remember to pick up her sticker or Ernie, the guard, would be on her tail. That's number ten on my list of things to do today, she thought ruefully, her heels tapping out a staccato rhythm on the parking lot's yellow-striped surface. In addition to doing the shopping and other catch-up chores necessary after being out of town for four weeks, there was her determination to make this first sports special *perfect*. The script approval with Jim Stafford had gone well the day before, and she was eager

19

to put the polishing touches on the editing and prove to the seasoned sportscaster what an asset she would be to the team.

She walked along the cobblestone path leading up to the broadcasting center, took a deep breath of spring air, and smiled. Yes, all was right with the world!

Golden daffodils and clumps of crocus peeked out from well-tended beds and mingled with the deep green ivy vines that crept across her pathway, over gnarled tree roots and up the sides of the building. WQEK was located in an older part of Lawrence, Kansas, near the university campus where Sally had received a graduate degree in broadcasting several years before. Lawrence had become home to Sally and she loved the small town with its oak-lined streets and gentle friendliness. She had done a brief stint on the campus station's staff, then moved quickly into a position at one of the town's commercial television stations where she had remained, moving rapidly up the ladder to her present position. And Lawrence had the added attraction of being less than an hour's drive from Kansas City, with the advantages of a larger metropolitan area, and the nursing home where her father resided.

Thinking once again of the many tasks of the day ahead of her, Sally quickened her gait, sending her blond hair flying. Every strand fell neatly back into place, amber floss cut in a soft bob. Sally had cut her hair short years ago, long before Lady Di burst upon the international scene. Sally still remembered the reaction of her on-again, off-again college beau, Hank Schuyler. He had had a fit. "What have you done with your hair, Sally? All those silken tresses," he ranted, sliding his hand over her suddenly naked neck and shoulders. ". . . and all that shimmering gold?"

"Used it to stuff a keepsake pillow," she had teased, laughing at his distress. "It's only hair, Hank, and I thought you rather liked my naked nape!" When others curled their hair into afros or grew it back in country-western waves, she ignored the trends and kept hers short. She enjoyed the crisp clean lines that framed her face, showing off her high cheekbones and the tapering curve of her neck. Now as she neared the double doors of WQEK, the sun-lightened strands tossed gently and the champagne highlights emphasized the golden tan of her shoulders and arms.

Sally moved through the large entrance and dashed with several others for the already closing doors of the elevator. Beaver and two of his camera crew were already inside, and he stuck one large blunt hand over the small circle of the electric eye. With a jerk and a threatening hum the door stopped in mid-slide and opened again.

"Come on," he laughed, elbowing the mustachioed fellow on his left. "Make room for the rest of the sardines!"

Sally eyed the cramped space and shook her head. "Not me, folks. Go on ahead. I'll catch the next one." She turned away and headed for the little newsstand tucked in a corner of the narrow lobby. Perched on a stool, wrapped in his familiar patched cardigan, was Davey the newsman.

"Well, good mornin', Sally me girl. I heard you were back but wouldn't believe it until I set eyes on your pretty face myself."

"Morning, Davey." Sally smiled warmly. "It's good to see you too! How are things?"

"Better than okay, lassie. And I sure enjoyed seeing you on TV every night down there in Florida. You looked mighty fine. You know, I was always missin' you when you were on at lunchtime, so I'm glad Mr. Slater knew a good thing when he saw it!"

"Me, too, Davey!" Sally grinned back. "And thanks for the vote of confidence."

"How did our boys look close up?"

"Just great, Davey. There's a new shortstop, and some new powerhouse hitters, and—"

"Good, good." The old man wrinkled his creased forehead. "But what a lousy break for our boy Decker."

There it was again! The sudden twitch inside her chest, the unexpected break in the rhythm of her pulse. Silly! she thought.

"Yes, just awful, Davey," she answered unemotionally. "But the team will come through. I think Decker overshadowed a lot of talent that will now emerge. You just wait and see. We're really looking good!"

"Okay, expert, think we'll make it to the series this year?"

"I'll bet on it, Davey!"

"Done, missy. Let's make it a fiver. And that's a bet it'll be a pleasure to lose!"

Sally laughed. Davey was always looking for a bet—on anything, with everyone. She'd lost count of how many times he had taken her money as he guessed how many pennies were in her pocketbook, what number spot she had parked in, or whether there were more than two zeros in the serial number on her dollar bill. She was still chuckling as she entered the mirrored elevator car, rode to the third floor, and stepped off, heading for the glass doors stenciled in block letters: NEWS WEATHER SPORTS.

Sally felt a shiver of pleasure. This was where she belonged . . . and she enjoyed every bit of it—from the wide oak desks, their tops buried under the clutter of copy and scripts, and the round disks of videotape, to the pale walls splashed with stills, the hastily scrawled notes in Slater's indecipherable hand, the schedules, agendas and the occasional words of praise from Harry Williams, the station manager, to the rush and bustle of the office clerks, the sharp ring of the phone, the clatter of teletypes and word processors . . . even the smell of the bitter coffee and Slater's ever-present cigars. Sally's skirt swirled up about her knees as she stepped through the door.

Returning the warm smiles and hellos, Sally headed for

her desk on the far side of the room. A stack of mail lay in the center and she lifted it with a practiced hand, thumbing quickly through the assortment of telegrams, envelopes, and brochures. She read the telegrams first— one from the Royals' coach thanking her for the professional coverage of spring training, another from an affiliate in Topeka asking to borrow a segment of one of her tapes. The brochures settled colorfully in the bottom of her wastebasket as she started in on the letters, opening the first as she walked over to the coffee machine.

She glanced up in surprise. "Goodness—what's going on this morning?"

Half a dozen people were clustered around the coffee maker and for the first time that morning Sally tuned in to the undercurrent of excitement in the air. "It's crazier than usual for a Tuesday morning. What have I missed?"

"I think that's what everyone's wondering," a news writer answered cryptically, then wandered off.

Sally poured her coffee, added a generous splash of cream, and walked over to Beaver's desk. "Beaver— what's up?"

"Not sure, Sal—but look around. Everyone has that harried expression last seen just before the threatened strike last year." He shrugged and winked. Then gave his curly beard a thoughtful tug. "Seems Williams himself was seen coming through here this morning on his way to Slater's office with his pipe already at full steam."

"Mr. Williams? Our esteemed station manager?"

"Yep—the head honcho himself. And when he left, word is Slater came out and he was as twitchy as a bitch in heat. He did three laps around the office, muttering things like baseball . . . ratings . . . prime time . . . and then vanished. You can see his heel marks in the carpet over there."

Automatically Sally followed the line of his pointing

23

finger, then laughed. "Beaver! You get me every time. But really, what do you think is going on?"

"Beats me, sugar . . . you're the sportscaster, and all the clues lead that-a-way. What do *you* think?"

Sally shook her head slowly. "I don't know, Beaver . . ." She walked thoughtfully back to her desk, the beginnings of a suspicion taking form in her mind. In her hand she held an honest-to-goodness piece of *fan* mail, from a station manager in Kansas City praising her on the excellent coverage of spring training and, she smiled to herself, on her own "inestimable charm"! And there had been several others, equally complimentary. Perhaps Mr. Williams had also been made aware of her success. Maybe— just maybe—he had been down to congratulate Bill Slater on his newest appointment.

The only female in the Denning family, Sally had been primed for this job all her twenty-six years. While other girls were learning how to curl their hair, she had approached adolescence with a baseball in one hand, a football in the other, and a baggy sweat shirt covering her softly swelling breasts. Sally's mother had died when her daughter was four, and although Sally mirrored Marie Denning's gentle beauty and literary bent, her father had gone to great lengths to see that she received all the same "advantages" as her all-star brother, be it Little League, baseball camp, or private batting lessons.

Suddenly the door to Slater's office flew open and a hush settled over the office. Sally's fingers tightened instinctively on the edge of her desk. Slater's gray eyes scanned the room and came to rest on Sally. "Well, Denning—I see you finally got here! Come into my office for a minute . . . please." An audible sigh escaped from those not summoned. One never knew from Slater's brusk manner whether they were to be feasted or fired. But Sally knew. With a wink at Beaver she followed her boss into the inner sanctum. "Coming, sir!"

Slater closed the door behind them. "Why don't you sit down, Sally? Here—the comfortable chair," he said, pulling an old leather armchair closer to his desk.

"Well, thank you, Mr. Slater. That's certainly royal treatment." Her eyes danced and a lovely smile lit her face.

"You deserve it, Sally." His usually gruff voice had softened. "You've done a fine job for us this spring. As I said yesterday, those clips from spring training were some of the best I've seen!"

"Thank you. Beaver's expertise was—"

"Yes, yes—I know. But you did a hell of a good job."

"Well, I am enjoying this job very much—"

"Yes, I know you are, Sally—I know it's all very important to you." His eyes shifted to the long sunlit rectangle of the window. Suddenly Sally was scared. The sweet taste of his praise had turned sour in her mouth. She crossed her arms over her chest and leaned back into the protective embrace of the chair.

"Bill?" Sally's voice was low and controlled. "Why do I have a terrible feeling there is a 'but' at the end of your sentence?"

"Now, Sally"—Slater turned back toward her, forcing a smile—"Sally . . . you have been, and *will* be, a most valuable asset to the sports staff here at WQEK. And there's no question about the quality of your work—"

"Then what *is* the question?" Sally started to interrupt but he waved her to silence.

"A most peculiar situation has arisen here at the station. Mr. Williams was in this morning to see me." He clasped his hands together and leaned toward her across the desk. "I have some good news and some bad . . ."

"I'll take the good, please," she quipped, feigning a calm she didn't feel.

"Now, Sally, don't rush me. You know that we're in the

25

middle of a ratings war with WMOT—that *is* the name of the game in broadcasting."

"I know that, and I also know that we're holding our own in those ratings."

"Yes!" he said, his voice rising. He waved a burned-out cigar stub in the air between them, punctuating each word. "Holding—our—own! But that is not good enough. And an opportunity has arisen that will send our ratings soaring!"

"An opportunity that involves me?" Sally asked, silently considering and rejecting a dozen possibilities that leaped to mind. "What has our great white chief come up with?"

"Sally," Slater cautioned, his brows furrowed, "I want you to hear me out before you say anything you'll regret. Just sit and listen for a minute." His gray eyes held hers. "You know that P. J. Decker was injured at spring training . . ."

Again—that man's name! Sally shuddered, suddenly flooded with an overwhelming feeling that if she turned around he would surely be standing behind her, or sitting out at her desk, or waiting around the corner. Why am I being haunted by this man I barely know—and, she said to herself, do not have any desire to know? She suppressed her irrational thoughts and managed a weak, "Yes . . . I know."

"Well, Decker will be back here in the area while he's recuperating—needs to be near the team doctors in K. C. You know he lives at Lake Winnepeg, a short twenty-five-minute drive from here."

Sally gripped the edge of her chair and forced back a reply. Why was Bill Slater sitting there, chewing his burned-out cigar, and chatting about P. J. Decker's choice of home locations? It made no sense to her. How she wished he'd pass over the idle chatter and let her know

26

why she was sitting there, plagued by an icy chill that was cross-country skiing down her spine.

". . . a fine man, that Decker." Sally tuned in to the end of the sentence and waited for Slater to continue. The large, burly man chewed over his words, then forced them out with a jerk. ". . . and Mr. Williams has talked him into doing the sportscasts with Stafford while he's recovering—"

Sally was out of her seat, her heart pounding beneath her soft sweater. All remnants of empathy for the ball player's plight had been instantly destroyed by Slater's last sentence. "What? No . . . no, Mr. Slater—that's not fair! Mr. Williams can't do that to me!"

"Sally—"

"No, he can't! That damn Decker!"

"Sally, it's not his fault. And Mr. Williams is only doing his job—"

"Doing *his* job? No! That's what I've been doing—*my* job—and I'm darn good at it! You said so yourself. But this . . . this isn't right—it isn't fair!"

"It's the business, Sally. You know that as well as I do. Ratings are everything."

"And what about people? Don't I count in this game at all?"

He stood to face her across the desk. "Of course you do, Sally. And that's why I wanted a chance to talk to you myself. To make sure you understand that this is only temporary—only until Decker gets back into action."

"Only until Decker . . ." She fought to keep the quaver out of her voice. "And what about me? What do I do while that glamour boy does *my* job?"

While Slater had seemed sympathetic before, now he looked truly embarrassed. "Well, Sally . . . you remember that cooking show we had planned for the winter, and then tabled . . ."

Sally pushed herself against the back of the chair as if

27

she'd been burned. Her hands were clenched into fists at her side. "Oh, no, you don't! There isn't any chance of that! Not me, Mr. Slater—no!"

"Sally . . ."

"Mr. Slater—I said no!"

"It's done, Sally. Now lower your voice." He gave her a moment, then continued. "It's done. You can take it . . . or leave it. But we have nothing else to offer you right now. That's the way it stands. I'm sorry."

Sally stood still for a moment. She shook her head, fighting to keep the tears locked behind her burning lids. Then she mustered the little pride she had left and asked softly, "And if I agree to do the cooking show . . . ?"

"Then as soon as Decker leaves, the sportscast is yours again. I promise."

"You *promise?*" She tried to suppress the outrage welling up inside her. "And I'm supposed to hang my career on that hook? You want me to wait quietly on the sidelines while my career, my future, are washed away?"

"Sally, that's not at all what I'd like, and you know it!"

"Then why didn't you fight for me, Mr. Slater?" Her moist eyes betrayed her. "Why didn't you . . ."

"The odds were against us, Sal, a hundred to one. It doesn't make any sense to fight the battle if the war's already been lost."

"No, no, of course not." Sally pressed her lips together into a straight line, knowing there was nothing left to say. She held his gaze for a moment more, then turned away, her chin held high. "There are a few more clips that need editing for Saturday's spring-training special. Shall I finish those up today or . . ."

"Please do, Sally. That is still your piece—and you can be proud of it."

"I am, Bill," she answered coolly, and turned to leave. Her hand tightened on the doorknob. "Oh, yes, I'll clean my desk off this afternoon . . . so it will be ready for the arrival of your superstar. Perhaps I should leave some flowers in a vase . . ."

"Now, Sally—"

"Oh, don't worry, Mr. Slater. I wasn't going to go to any great expense." She lifted one arched eyebrow. "I was thinking of something simple and appropriate—like poison ivy!"

Bill grinned and winked encouragingly. "That a girl, Sally. I knew this wouldn't throw you off your stride."

"No, no, there's no need to worry about me. I'm fine and dandy." She took a deep breath, squared her shoulders, and turned the knob.

The knob stuck, then fought back. It turned within her hand, twisting her wrist and fingers. Then the door was pushed open from the outside. Its edge caught her on the shoulder, offsetting her balance. She stumbled and fell back against a row of filing cabinets. For a brief moment her vision clouded and the room swam before her eyes.

"Miss—are you all right?" Two strong hands lifted her upright. She could feel them smoothing the sleeves of her sweater, tightening warmly on her elbows. "Are you all right?" the vaguely familiar voice asked again.

Sally nodded and took a tentative step toward the door and stumbled. Once again the stranger was there supporting her, leaning her against his wide chest to catch her breath. She could feel the warmth of his body, his shirt brushing against her cheek. He smelled like the outdoors —pine trees and fresh-mowed grass. After the strain of the past few moments, she felt strangely secure, relaxed; the tension she had felt all morning drained away. This was so nice, she didn't *want* to fight battles anymore. What foolish thoughts! Angry with herself, she forced her head off his shoulder and looked up. His eyes were cocoa brown, soft and warm as a spaniel's and filled with concern.

"There, that's better. You had me worried for a minute. You're okay?"

Sally nodded weakly, lost in the depths of those brown eyes, the warm cocoon of his voice. "I . . . I'm fine. It was my fault, I wasn't paying attention." She rubbed the back of one hand over her eyes, trying to clear the cotton batting from her brain.

He was looking at her strangely. "I thought the door was stuck, and sometimes I forget my own strength," he apologized again.

"Don't apologize." Sally pulled gently back from the circle of his arms. "I'm . . ." Her eyes flew wide. "P. J. Decker!"

The man opposite her was obviously used to surprised reactions from women. "No, *I'm* P. J. Decker," he responded with a cool, practiced grin. "And *you're?*" Then the grin vanished and his face mirrored her surprise. He shook his head in disbelief, and before Sally could move, he reached out and cupped her chin in a surprisingly gentle roughly calloused hand. "It *is* you, isn't it . . . Florence Nightingale!" He was smiling now, an expression of pure pleasure lighting his face. "It really *is* you. I never thought I'd see you again."

Sally was awash with embarrassment. Out of the corner of her eye she could see the astonished expressions on the faces of her boss and Harry Williams. Quickly, as though shooing away a pesky mosquito, she brushed his hand from her face. "Mr. Decker . . ."

"Wait a minute, I'm not wrong, am I?"

"No, but . . ."

"Why didn't you ever come back?"

"I did." She looked uncomfortably over at the two men watching and lowered her voice. "I did, but you had plenty of company."

"But I wanted to thank you." His eyes twinkled. I even had Joey, Joey Rao, out looking for you—"

30

"Please, Mr. Decker . . ."

"Wait a minute, what are *you* doing here?"

"I *work* here!" With an exasperated shrug she slipped out of his reach and leaned back against the cold, uncomplicated wall.

Bill Slater filled the awkward silence. "Well, what a nice coincidence. Sally hadn't mentioned that she knew you." He glanced reproachfully at Sally, then added, "But that's a nice little bonus. We're all a team here at WQEK."

And it's about time we got to the business at hand!" Harry Williams stepped forward and draped a heavy arm around Sally's slim shoulders, drawing her out of the center of the group. "First things first, P. J. This gentleman here is your new boss, Bill Slater. Best damn news producer in the Midwest!" Bill reddened under the profuse praise as he shook the ball player's hand. Williams continued, "Bill is pleased as punch to have you on the team, P. J. Can't wait to see those ratings soar, right, men?" He laughed and Sally caught the message when his grip tightened on her shoulder. When he turned her toward the two men, she forced a small smile. "And this lovely lady, whom you seemed to have met, is Sally Denning. She wears lots of hats here at WQEK, right, Sally? She's going to be doing a new cooking show for us this season called . . . uh, what's that thing called, Bill?"

"*The Back Burner,* Harry."

"Oh, right! Doesn't that sound great?" Again the pressure tightened slightly on her soft skin.

Sally nodded and drew free of his grasp. "Yes, well I had better get back to work . . ."

P. J. stepped forward, blocking her quick exit, and took her hand. As her palm melted into his she felt the resulting charge travel up the nerves of her arm. Annoyed with herself, she tried to pull her hand away.

"It certainly was a pleasure being officially introduced, Sally Denning. How about lunch? Perhaps you could show me around. It would give me a chance to apologize for knocking you off your feet."

His dark eyes flashed with humor. Or was that a hint of mockery in his smile? She let her fingers go limp within his hand and cocked one hip. "Well, city buses and Saint Bernards have the same effect, but *this* was merely an accident." Before the beat of her pulse and the sudden dampness of her skin could betray her, she drew her hand away. Anger and humor had always been her surest allies. She wrapped both about her like a cloak and with a self-assured smile she said, "I'm sure Mr. Williams would prefer to show you around. Now if you gentlemen will excuse me"—she turned toward the door—"I think I smell something burning."

CHAPTER TWO

The cloud of anger and gloom around Sally gradually grew to such proportions that the news staff finally left her alone. She snapped at Beaver and walked away whenever Robin approached. Even Slater backed off, deciding this was something she'd have to work out by herself. He knew she'd eventually see this was the best thing for the station, and then everything would once again settle down to the usual controllable confusion.

But not in Sally's feverish mind. She shuffled papers, slammed drawers shut, pulled out tapes, then shoved them back into their slots. "Damn!" she muttered to herself over and over again as the day wore on and the afternoon sun dropped, casting dark shadows through the long newsroom windows. "Damn P. J. Decker! Damn baseball! Damn TV!"

"Listen everyone." Bill Slater's deep voice broke through the newsroom and pierced Sally's self-imposed exile and comforting curses. "I need your attention for a moment. Sorry this is such short notice but Mr. and Mrs. Williams are having a fancy 'do' tonight to which you are all invited. The party is in honor of our newest member of the staff who will officially join our ranks tomorrow. It is Mr. and Mrs. Williams's expressed wish that we all make P. J. Decker feel as welcome and comfortable here as possible. Naturally, the media will be there—can't hurt those ratings any." He laughed loudly, casting a nervous glance in Sally's direction. "We need to milk this temporary star attraction for all we can, you know." He paused, looked around at his audience, then added, "Well—that's it. Eight o'clock at the Williams's home, and *everyone* is expected to attend." Then, before anyone could reply, he turned and walked abruptly back into his office, slamming the door behind him.

There was silence for a moment, then a few hushed comments which turned to laughter and excited exclamations. "Fantastic . . ." "Oh, to get close to that hunk . . ." "Imagine, dancing on the Williams's patio with the sexiest man in baseball!" The women's comments filled the air and even the men were looking forward to a chance to converse with the baseball great. Only Sally sat in silence, her face grim. Unnoticed, she stuffed a stack of papers into her portfolio, grabbed her purse, and headed across the room. Robin turned just as Sally opened the newsroom door. "Bye, Sally—see you tonight," she called excitedly.

"That I doubt!" Sally retorted and flew down the hall toward the elevators.

Beaver reached her just as the heavy doors slid open. He stretched one arm across the opening to block her way and looked into her troubled face. "Sally, this isn't like you at all. *You're* our stalwart, the one who helps everyone else shrug off disappointments. I know this is a rotten break, kiddo. But don't put your career on the line because of a minor setback."

"Beaver, it's more than that. It's the whole situation."

"I know, Sal. It's having a macho star be the one to push you out on the doorstep for a while. It's—"

"It's knowing I can do as good a job, if not *better,* than he can!"

"That's not quite fair, Sally. You've never even seen him in action."

"Oh, no? I've seen what he can do on the field and heard plenty of reports about his prowess *off* the field. And although both of *those* performances may earn him superstar status, neither one qualifies him for *my* job! I worked long and hard to get here and I'm proud of myself . . ." Her voice trailed off weakly. "And other people are proud of me."

Beaver dropped a hand to her shoulder. "You're worried about your dad, aren't you? Listen, I know Lou. He'd be proud of his daughter if you decided to push brooms for a living."

"Beaver, you don't understand. Please, let's drop it."

"Maybe I don't understand. But I am a friend. And I do care about you. I won't let you risk your job because you're busy trying to make a point. If you don't show up at Williams' tonight, it'll be read as a personal affront to Decker. And Williams would take your job—*all* our jobs —for a whole lot less! So, my dear, I'll pick you up at seven forty-eight sharp. Be dazzlin' and show them all what the Denning clan is made of!" He let go of the doors, turned, and walked back toward the newsroom.

Sally moved slowly and thoughtfully across the tiny living room that was the center of her third-floor apartment. The room was comfortable and intriguing and very much Sally. It was filled with books, paintings, and photographs she had collected over the past few years. Most of the comfortable furniture was salvaged from the large family home in Kansas City she had closed four years before. Her eyes came to rest on a large framed photograph atop the polished oak mantelpiece.

It was a formal, posed family portrait taken in her

father's wood-paneled den. Marie Denning stood next to her husband, a small, blond baby girl held lovingly in her arms. Her erect posture and fine features gave her an almost regal appearance. Her eyes were shining, intense, and filled with kindness. Sally stared at her for a moment, filled with love for this woman she had never really known. How strange blood ties are, she thought. Overpowering at times . . . they guide you, control you. Her eyes shifted to her brother, Matt, standing at her father's side, a baseball clutched tightly in his gloved hand. So tall and handsome. He had his mother's eyes, his father's determined jaw, and his own indomitable spirit. He had been Sally's hero for as long as she could remember. And even at the age of ten he had looked so proud and bold standing there, chin raised, gazing into the future.

Sally drew a deep, steadying breath. "It's okay," she whispered to herself. "P. J. Decker is just a small setback. Beaver was right. It will take more than a hotshot baseball player to dampen the Denning spirit."

The sound of Beaver's muffler-damaged jeep on the shaded street below interrupted Sally's thoughts and she moved to the long walnut mirror near the doorway. Smoothing her hair in place, she smiled at her reflection and opened the door as a huffing-puffing Beaver fell over the doorstep.

"Sally, when are you going to talk that landlady into an elevator? This over-thirty body can't take too much of—" He stopped and stared at Sally, drawing in a deep breath, then expelling it in a shrill whistle, as he stood back. "Wow! You are *gorgeous!*"

And indeed she was. Sally had brushed her golden hair to a burnished gloss, the varied tawny hues lying in thick waves about her face and around the curve of her neck. She wore a shimmering midnight-blue taffeta blouse that ruffled about the back of her neck. The plunging neckline barely concealed the soft globes of her breasts. A wide belt

36

emphasized her tiny waistline and the fullness of the blue and silver skirt that floated about her hips and thighs. She wore narrow strapped sandals of the same deep blue color, their spiked heels lending her a long, leggy appearance. A touch of color on her high smooth cheeks and across her lips completed her outfit. She curtsied playfully. "You approve?"

Beaver was silent for a moment as his eyes appreciated the sight before him. As he nodded his full approval, he looked into her face, admiration and amusement sparking his eyes. "I see you've packed all your ammunition tonight."

Sally blushed slightly and held open the door. "The only way to go, Beaver my friend, the only way to go."

Sally and Beaver turned up the long circular drive leading to the Williams' many-acred estate. Tiny gaslights flickered along the drive's edge, highlighting the towering Tudor mansion and the carefully manicured gardens. Stars twinkled overhead in the midnight-blue sky and a cool breeze wafted through the open sides of the jeep.

Sally had been to the Williams' home twice before and both times left with a bloated feeling. Filled with too much opulence, too many riches displayed throughout the twenty-one-room mansion, and too many hovering servants. She often thought Harry Williams would have been more comfortable in an old hunting jacket and worn boots, but instead he allowed Adelle Williams, the owner of WQEK, her frills and fancies and social extravaganzas, while he efficiently managed the station and patiently stood at her side in his tuxedo and tails to be photographed for the society pages.

Beaver, waving away the valet's offer, parked the jeep himself, and he and Sally walked toward the brightly lit house. The swell of elegantly dressed guests had already gathered under the front portico.

The air brushing Sally's cheeks and lips was heavy with

37

the spring smells of budding greenness and awakening earth. The well-tended flower bed glistened with crystal water drops from a recent sprinkling. Each swelling bud seemed diamond encrusted in the flickering light of the gaslamps. Sally drew a deep steadying breath as she and Beaver climbed the wide steps to the front door. A uniformed butler greeted them, ushered them inside, and made certain each had a glass of champagne before returning to his post.

"Adelle threw this little fête together in one day?" Sally murmured, surveying the elaborate party trappings. There seemed to be dozens of frilly-aproned waitresses balancing trays of steaming hors d'oeuvres while the dance band and a few couples shared the polished parquet floor at the far end of the living room.

"I think she keeps all the trimmings stored in a closet and just carts it out on cue," Beaver joked. "Including the twenty-piece band."

They grinned at each other and walked past the wide, curving staircase toward the main salon.

Heavy silk drapes stirred at the open windows, rich carpets muffled their steps, and gleaming crystal chandeliers threw bright light into every corner. No lingering shadows or softly lit corners for Mr. and Mrs. Williams. How different from the cozy old home of her childhood, Sally thought.

As they entered the room, Sally felt a wave of appraising glances wash over her. This was the moment she had dreaded. The looks, the knowing glances, the pity for poor Sally who got pushed out of the spotlight and into the kitchen! But what she saw astounded her. Yes, they were all watching her, but the glances were complimentary. The men's eyes filled with the surprised look of the hunter who had just spotted his first deer, the women were more companionably admiring. She had always been a favorite at the station and now she was surrounded by the fortifying proof of that esteem. They were on her side. Smiling and chatting, she joined the welcoming group around the polished grand piano.

A commotion near the wide doors drew the attention of all in the room back toward the entranceway. The guest of honor had arrived. P. J. Decker stood in the doorway, his large handsome frame a study in ease and self-confidence. Despite the bulge where his shoulder was still taped and strapped, he looked like Madison Avenue's idea of sportsman of the year. A silky cream-colored shirt covered his torso, outlining the hidden muscles beneath the thin fabric. He wore dark slacks, and Sally's eyes were unwillingly drawn to the curve of the athlete's muscles across his hips and thighs. Again she felt the strength—compelling, dangerous—of his sensuality. Her blood pounded in her head and her throat tightened painfully. It's only anger, she chided herself. But every nerve ending called her liar. Like a separate entity, her body clamored at the mere sight of him.

Their eyes met. A flush spread across her neck and cheeks. She had been staring at him, and he knew it, accepted it, acknowledged it. His lips curved in that amused, inviting smile she was getting to know all too well, and his eyes tantalized. With an effort of will, she pulled her gaze away and turned to the young newspaper man standing next to her around the curve of the piano's frame.

"So, Henry, what do you think of the situation in the Middle East?"

"Rotten. As always. I like the local news a lot better tonight. What I wouldn't give to be in that fellow's shoes."

Sally drummed nervously on the polished wood. "Is that all anyone can talk about today?"

"Do you have any better suggestions?" he retorted. Then a smile returned. "Hey, here they come now!"

Stay away, stay away! Sally prayed silently, her hands

still on the piano's edge. As though pulled by a magnet, the small conspicuous group with P. J. at its core headed directly for her. For the slightest fraction of a second Sally toyed with the urge to run and hide, but instead arranged her face in what she hoped was a bright, aloof smile and turned to face them.

"Good evening, Mrs. Williams."

"Good evening, Sally dear. Mr. Decker, I would like you to meet Sally Denning, one of our most talented staff members."

P. J. accommodatingly stuck out his hand, a grin splitting his face. Sally was forced to respond. The moment he had captured her fingers he offered a mock half bow over her hand. Sally tried to pull her hand back, afraid he was actually going to kiss her and embarrass them both to death. She could have murdered him where he stood. That maddening smile, those laughing brown eyes. Slowly he lifted his head. Sally could feel his eyes outlining the curves of her hips and waist, her breasts, her neck. She could trace their path by the fiery tingling of her skin. She felt aroused, exposed, and suddenly defenseless. "We have already met, Mrs. Williams, thank you," she murmured, pulling her hand free.

The older woman now looked totally confused. "You have? Oh, dear, then why . . . ?"

"It's my fault, Mrs. Williams," P. J. interrupted, his charm soothing every ruffled feather. "I just wanted another opportunity to hold Miss Denning's hand. And I'd hoped you would put in a good word for me." He patted the plump hand resting on his arm and winked conspiratorially.

Her full face reddening under her makeup, Mrs. Williams winked back. "Now, now, P. J. If I were doing my duty, I think I would be offering Sally warnings rather than encouragement." Her high-pitched laugh mingled with his deep, throaty chuckle.

"Unfair, Mrs. Williams."

"Ah, but all's fair . . ."

Sally had heard enough. Too much! In a moment they'd have her signed, sealed, and delivered! "Excuse me. It was quite an honor seeing you again, Mr. Decker, and you can rest assured further introductions will not be necessary. I *won't* forget you!" She glared at him with as much fierceness as she could muster, then turned to her hostess. "Mrs. Williams, thank you for inviting me to this lovely party. I'm having a wonderful time. If you'll both excuse me for a moment, I think I'll find something to nibble on."

Robin was standing near the buffet table and Sally stalked to her side. "Hi, Robin."

"Well, hi there, Sally. Isn't this swell? Here, try some of these stuffed oysters."

Sally bit gingerly into the edge of one of the shivering morsels.

"Aren't they marvelous? But the best thing in sight just walked into that room," Robin teased, pointing over her shoulder. "Oh, P. J. Decker is so yummy. I've never seen a silk shirt look so good. Only baseball players and dancers look that good from behind. I'd like to get my hands on that for a while."

"Robin, you're crazy! He's just another man. Besides, there are plenty in line ahead of you."

"No problem. I like a challenge!" Robin grinned and popped a stuffed olive into the round red circle of her mouth.

Sally rolled her eyes upward and fought the laugh that tickled her throat. "You are *no* help at all, Robin."

"Oh, sorry, Sally!" The younger girl gasped. "I really forgot. I bet that super stud's not on your top-ten list today. But a good broadcaster is supposed to be objective, right? And you *are* good; we all know that, even Mr. Williams." She snapped playfully to attention, then leaned back against the table. "So try not to worry. You'll be back on at six o'clock before you know it, and in the meantime why not make the best of a bad situation?" She winked, speared another olive, and sashayed off across the room.

Sally sighed. Why not? Why not just make peace? But, she thought, drawing a narrow hand across her brow, that would mean mastering this muddle of emotion I seem to have become. Oh, damn! She hit the edge of the table with the flat of her hand and the crystal platters and bowls and the silver spoons burst into a noisy chorus. Sally jumped back, shrugged apologetically at those who had turned to stare, and fled from the room.

The nearest exit was a set of French doors opening onto the garden. Sally stepped through, crossed the wide brick patio, and rushed on down the cobbled path into the darkness. The lights of the house disappeared behind her, screened by the manicured yew hedge and the grove of paper birch, their thin new leaves rustling above her head. As she walked on, a pale light, ghostly but beautiful, seemed to rise from the garden itself. "A reflection from the stars, perhaps," Sally mused aloud, feeling the tension drain away, the sweet stillness of the night soothing her. She bent to pluck a blade of new grass and put it between her lips. It tasted cool, sweet and fresh. The perfect oval shapes of the azaleas lined the walk, their gray-black branches softened and rounded by the first plumage of leaves. There was no hint yet of the extravagant burst of color locked within, only the small humped shapes along her way. Between them here and there the ground was cracked, pushed aside by the impatient leaves of the earliest tulips. Sally followed the path, stepping carefully around a tiny stone cherub set at the walkway's edge. When the path detoured around the base of an ancient oak, its trunk encircled by a stone bench, she sat down. The back of the bench was curved and Sally let her head loll back and closed her eyes. Above her a bird called, and then another, and from a far-off branch a mockingbird began to sing, spilling out into the darkness the music he had gathered all day long. The sound drifted around her like moondust. Then suddenly it was silent. Sally opened her eyes and slipped forward to the edge of the bench. What had disturbed the bird? Some animal? Someone? She peered back up the path, then sat bolt upright as a deep voice cursed in the night.

"Damn! Ow! Where'd that come from?" The muttered growl grew closer, and Sally's eyes widened in fear. They narrowed into angry slits as P. J. Decker stepped, or rather limped, into view.

"There you are! Did you have to hike so far in the middle of the night?"

"Did I have to . . . ? What are you talking about? And what in the world are you doing out here?"

"Me? I followed you," he answered with that maddening touch of amusement in his voice. "So really, this is all *your* fault." He hobbled over to the bench, favoring his right leg, and dropped down beside her.

Sally was immediately aware of the warm length of his thigh next to hers. She edged down the bench but P. J. merely shifted his body and brought them back into electrifying contact again.

His eyes were full of boyish innocence when he looked into hers. "Don't you want me to tell you what happened?"

"Tell me what happened," she repeated, her voice more gentle than she had intended.

He had that boyish look again, but this time with his mouth down in a pout. "I tripped over something out there in the dark. Think I broke my toe." He crossed his right leg over the left, slipped off his shoe, and wiggled his sock-covered toes. "What do you think? Broken?"

Sally sat rigid, her hands in her lap.

"Come on, Florence Nightingale. It really hurts! Give

43

a guy a break." He nudged her coaxingly with his sore shoulder.

Begrudgingly, Sally reached across his lap and rubbed the proffered foot. There was something unexplicably erotic about the feel of the soft, warm wool beneath her palm, and when he wiggled his toes again, she giggled. "Stop that!"

"Why? I thought you'd need to see them in action."

"You're impossible," she shook her head. "But I don't think anything is broken."

"Then maybe my luck has changed." He grinned wryly, and there was a barely noticeable edge to his voice. "Seems like ever since the accident . . . It's crazy, but all of a sudden, I feel clumsy, off balance, you know? Bumping into things. Tripping in the dark. Then I knocked *you* down this morning!" He swallowed. "I was really afraid I had hurt you."

"It wasn't your fault," Sally insisted.

He flashed that beautiful smile again. "You know, though, when I picked you up and felt your head against my shoulder, my arms around you, I just had the feeling my luck had changed."

Sally watched his face, fascinated. What beautiful, soft eyes, she thought. Deep and gentle, like a puppy's. And the smooth, clean curve of his mouth. She shook her head, trying to clear away those wild, unbidden thoughts. Sally Denning, this is P. J. Decker sitting here, the man who . . .

"Don't you want to know why I followed you?"

"Yes." She nodded firmly. "That's right! What were you doing following me anyway? You have no right."

"I brought you a present."

"You what?"

"Yup. It's waiting out there, next to whatever jumped out and bit my foot."

"The angel."

44

"What?"

"An angel. A little stone angel," she explained, then teased mockingly. "You weren't looking where you were going."

"No. I was following my own angel." His voice was a husky purr and he leaned closer, his eyes caressing her face. "A pistachio-eyed angel at that! How interesting."

Sally pulled back against the bench, and as she did her breasts brushed lightly against his arm. Her nipples tautened and tiny electric sparks radiated through her body. This is getting out of hand! Struggling for self-control, she drew away and tightened up.

"Don't go away, Sally." Again, that sensual purr.

"Mr. Decker, I . . ."

"Mr. Decker? What's that for? What have I done, Sally, that always makes you so angry? Hell, you were angry the minute you set eyes on me. What did I do?"

"I'll tell you exactly what you did! You showed up with your cocky attitude and your inflated ego and took *my* job!"

His eyes went blank beneath furrowed brows. Then, as she continued, understanding filled them.

"That's right. What did you think, that one minute I was out covering sports and the next I was begging to do that little cooking show? Sure! You probably think all women should be wearing aprons and doing nice little housewifely things."

"Now, hold on. That's not at all what—"

"No, you asked! Now, just listen. That was *my* job, my first shot at sportscasting, and I worked hard for it. I spent two years doing noon broadcasts interviewing gynecologists and dress designers, hair stylists and herpes experts. And I finally got the job as Stafford's coanchor. Then *you* show up and . . ."

His hands fell heavy on her shoulders. "Now wait just one minute!" His grip was strong, not strong enough to be

45

painful, but strong enough for Sally to know he meant it. "Hold it just one minute, Ms. Denning. Number one, I didn't come asking for this job. Williams came to me. Number two, *I'd* rather be out there on the field. Oh, would I. Out there making sports news, not recording it. And number three, I didn't know whose job this was, or that it was *anyone's* job. I thought he just put me on as an extra to give the good folks out there a thrill. But maybe, just maybe, if I had known it was yours—if I had known *you* before and how important it all seems to be to you— maybe I would have said no. I could have sat around and done deodorant commercials, or"—a hint of sparkle returned to his eyes—"or paraded across America's living rooms in Fruit of the Loom. But I *didn't* know. I'm sorry, but it is not my fault."

Sally sat with his hands on her shoulders. Her anger was being swept away in a flood of other emotions, ranging from shame to desire. When she shivered, he drew his hands up and down her arms, chasing the chill away.

"Sorry I yelled," he said after a long silent moment.

"I'm sorry too."

"Friends?"

She nodded, afraid to test her voice.

"Okay, then please *don't* call me Mr. Decker again. That tone could kill. Promise?" His brows lifted questioningly.

"Promise, P. J." she said tentatively.

"Nope! That's no good, either. Day in, day out I've got people calling P. J. 'P. J., I need somethin'.' 'P. J. I want somethin'.' 'P. J., you're not good enough!' 'P. J. you're the greatest!' Nope! Not you. Let's try Peter. That's what I was called growing up. It was the media that dubbed me P. J."

Sally formed the word with her lips and tongue. "Peter." She tasted it as she said it, savoring it. "Peter Decker."

46

"That's nice," he nodded. "Yeah, that's just fine, Sally Denning. Nice to meet you." In the evening shadows Sally could see the crinkles of smile lines around his eyes, the unmarked smoothness of his skin over his jaw, the pale white line of an old scar crossing his left brow. She was delighted to see he had a dimple. Without thinking she lifted a forefinger and touched his cheek. He turned his face and caught her fingertip between his teeth. His lips were cool and moist, his tongue rough and rasping against the soft, sensitive skin of her fingertip.

With a gasp Sally pulled her hand away and the rapid sound of her breathing echoed in her ears. Anticipating his next move, she watched him warily.

But instead of kissing her, Peter Decker leaned back against the bench, returning her gaze from beneath lowered lids. A small smile played over his lips. "I think this is a good time to give you your present." In one fluid motion he rose to his feet and headed back up the path. "Wait there! Don't vanish on me now, angel." The darkness hid him for a moment and then he was back with two tulip shaped glasses clinking together in one hand and an unopened bottle of champagne in the other.

Without a word he handed Sally the glasses. In the moonlight the crystal sparkled like sunlight on water, and she held them up before her, marveling at their beauty. The loud pop of the cork made her jump, and they both laughed. The amber champagne was foaming with bubbles and Sally sniffed the sweet grape smell.

"No. That's not the way," Peter teased. With one hand under her elbow, he lifted her to her feet. Then he extended his glass in a toast. "To you . . . and me . . . and the whims of fortune."

The glasses chimed; the sound fell in drifts between them, around them.

The champagne had warmed and the bubbles tickled.

Sally gulped the glassful, then rubbed the back of one hand across her nose.

Peter laughed. "I can see I've got a teetotaler on my hands here. You'd never make it in the baseball circuit. Here." He refilled her glass, then dug into one pocket and drew forth a crumpled cocktail napkin. The edges unfolded, revealing a stash of salty, red-skinned Spanish peanuts. "Nibble a few of these to take the edge off."

Sally plucked a handful and grinned. "Do you always carry dinner around in your pocket? What else have you got in there?"

Without a moment's hesitation he turned one slim hip toward her invitingly. "Why don't you reach in and find out? Go ahead."

"Oh, no!" Sally laughed. "I don't think I'm ready for any more surprises tonight."

With a throaty laugh Peter took the two glasses and set them on the bench. Then he drew her to him, his arm holding her close, captive.

As though she needed that restraint. The very nearness of his body held her spellbound. Where the champagne had seeped through her, loosening her muscles and stirring her blood, now the heat of his body melted her bones, turned her blood to liquid fire. The yielding softness of her breasts pressed against the hard wall of his chest. Her nipples hardened, aching with sudden sensitivity. Deep within her the currents of desire pooled and spread. Her knees were weak and she leaned her weight against his hips and thighs. His body meshed with hers, supporting her easily.

She heard that throaty laugh again. Sally tilted her face to his, and he bent and kissed her. His lips brushed softly against hers. Their touch was no more than a moth's wings, but she could taste the salt and the sweetness on his lips. He turned his face and kissed her hairline, trailing kisses across her face. His lips traced the curve of her ear;

48

his teeth tugged gently at the sensitive curve of her lobe. As he nuzzled her, his breath lifted the floss on her neck, sending shivers up and down her spine.

Sally lifted onto tiptoe, wrapping both arms around Peter's neck. Her desire lay heavy on her, unexpected but undeniable. There was no resisting the pent-up depths of emotion she had long held dammed within her. The anger, the hunger, and the denial were all released in a lusty torrent. She let her head fall back and Peter's mouth sought the soft hollow of her neck. He rubbed warm lips against her skin, licking at the concave cup of her throat. His tongue was velvet, stroking her.

A soft cry gathered in Sally's throat and Peter's body responded. His muscles tightened, hardened, and tensed to the point of pain. His mouth lifted from her throat and his lips found hers. His mouth opened over hers, forcing her lips apart. His tongue slipped into the warm, sweet cave of her mouth and he drank the nectar he found there.

Sally didn't want ever to breathe if it meant an end to this. She savored the taste and smell of him. Lifting one hand she ran her fingers through his thick hair and caught a handful in her fist. She kissed him hungrily, nibbling, her sharp teeth catching the tender flesh of his lips, biting oh, so gently. With a moan he slipped his hands beneath her skirt's waistband, and up under her blouse. His hands roamed free over her back. The rough calluses on his fingertips and palms excited her. The slightly abrasive feel was delicious against the silken smoothness of her skin. His touch drifted up and down her spine, traced the curved pattern of her ribs, then lingered teasingly over her stomach. Sally drew in her breath, then released it in a slow, shuddering sigh as his hands found the soft curve of her breasts. He cupped the silken mounds in his palms and with maddening slowness rotated his thumb over her nipple. She responded in a way she had never known before.

"Oh, Peter," she whispered into his hair. The rough pad

of his thumb worked deliciously on her flesh, the tip of her breast now straining against the waterlike feel of the material separating her body from his.

With a sound that mirrored her passion, Peter pulled her roughly against him, pressing his hard length against her. "Sally . . . my sweet Sally," he groaned. "I've wanted you from the minute I saw you. From the first touch of your hand on my face. Sally . . . let's leave here. Come home with me."

She tried to ignore his voice and concentrate only on the wonderful feel of his body.

But he was persistent, urging. "Sally, please. Let me make love to you."

With an angry jerk she pulled free of his touch. Was that all this wonderful kiss was? Just a preliminary. Just a warm-up exercise for the big game. Just batting practice? "No, Peter. I . . . I . . ." She fought the tremor in her voice, then fumbled with the loose edge of her blouse, stuffing it angrily back into place.

"Sure. Go on. Tuck everything back in, all neat and in place." His voice shook with emotion. "Is that you, Sally? Turn it on, then off when it pleases you?"

"How dare you?" Her eyes flashed with fury. "What do you know about me anyway?"

"Nothing!" His voice softened. "Not enough. But I *want* to. I want to know everything about you. What makes you so soft and lovely, so angry, so sad."

That hurt. Sally spun away, careful to stay out of reach of his caressing hand. "That's none of your business, Mr. Decker. I'm my own person!"

"That doesn't mean . . ."

"What it means is that I want you to leave me alone. All this sweet talk. The sudden concern. Do you always go to such elaborate lengths to get a woman into bed?"

"If I *want* one in bed, I usually don't have to go to any lengths at all. It's keeping them *out* that's the problem."

50

"Oh, I can see I've wounded that fragile male pride."

"Lady, I've—"

"So, now it's lady. Well, just remember this. If you're looking for someone to keep your bed warm during your brief employment in our fair town, look somewhere else!"

Decker glared at her for a moment, his hands clenched at his sides, his face white. Then he bent down, picked up one glass, and threw it hard against the trunk of the old oak. The shattered pieces fell like a thousand tiny mirrors on the path around their feet. Sally stared stubbornly down at them as the harsh sound of his footsteps faded up the path.

She almost tripped over Robin as she stepped back onto the patio moments later.

"You? Was it you, Sally? Out there alone with P. J. Decker? I couldn't believe it. He came stomping past here like bee-stung bear. What happened?"

"His game was rained out." Sally sighed, sinking wearily onto the top step.

CHAPTER THREE

Things went smoothly for P. J. Decker as he slipped effortlessly into Sally's niche on the evening's sports broadcasts. Too smoothly, she thought. Viewers warmed to his gentle humor, deep brown eyes, and baseball expertise, and almost immediately the ratings began to edge their way up the scale.

Sally dutifully busied herself polishing up the weekend sports special as she had promised. She managed to avoid close contact with P. J., although his husky voice and warm laughter floated through the halls and tugged at her senses as she slipped in and out of the studios. But she couldn't avoid seeing him at the other end of a hallway, sitting on the news set, at morning planning sessions. She mustered polite hellos and smiles, not trusting her emotions for further dialogue. Nope, Sally, don't get involved, she counseled herself again and again. We're from two different worlds. Being another notch on P. J. Decker's bat isn't exactly a part of my life or career plans! Although P. J. Decker kept his distance, she knew his eyes were on her as she walked down the halls. She felt his gaze caress her like heat from a fire as she went through the newsroom and sat across from him at meetings.

By Friday Sally had the sports special polished to a professional shine. Reluctantly she handed the scripts and tapes over to Jim Stafford and bid her work farewell.

"Treat this well, Jim. I feel a little bit like I'm giving up a child for adoption!"

"Will do, Sal. From what I've seen, you can be very proud of this. We'll do it right, I promise! Now, when do we get to see you in action with the pots and pans?"

Sally grimaced. "As a matter of fact, I'm about to venture into the hostile terrain right now. Robin is meeting me for some preliminaries on the set, and we'll have our first show Monday at noon. Heartburn à la Sally Denning!"

Jim laughed. "Can't wait! And, Sal, it's awfully nice to see that sparkle back in those beautiful eyes."

Sally smiled and exited from the sportscaster's office, proud of her job at emotional camouflage. She made her way slowly down the long corridor leading to the cooking set. At the end of the hall she paused and glared at a sign above two heavy glass doors: The Back Burner—Set 3. "That's where I've been stowed all right, on the back burner!" she muttered under her breath, and pushed her lean body through the doors, letting them swing shut behind her. Cautiously she stepped onto the set and surveyed the scene before her. A cheery, well-equipped kitchen filled the tiny set. Shiny copper pots and pans hung from a decorative wrought-iron rack above the orderly cooking island that was filled with kitchen gadgets of every size and shape. Sally walked closer and stared at her reflection in the polished stainless steel appliances lining the counter top. "Good Lord, do I feel *that* terrible?" she mumbled, pushing the heavy food processor to one side and flopping her papers down on the butcher block surface.

"Isn't this terrific, Sally?" Robin burst through a side door, her red hair flying in the breeze. "It's a gourmet's dream!"

"And *my* nightmare!" Sally retorted. She pulled out a tall stool from beneath the counter, sat down, and wound her slender legs around it. "Oh, Robin. I look at all these neat, shiny, self-possessed little machines"—she waved at the row of food processors, mixers, blenders, and toasters —"and I feel as if they're *laughing* at me. They *know*, Robin. I swear to God they do!"

Robin giggled at the desperation in her friend's voice. "Come on, Sal, you can do it. Is there *anything* you've tried that hasn't turned out A-okay? I doubt it!" She confidently answered her own question, then continued, "Mr. Slater sent for me earlier today. Since Alice Johnson is still ill, we need a producer for *The Back Burner*. I am about to get my first chance at producing something single-handedly. What do you think of that?"

Sally laughed, feeling more relaxed. "Terrific. We'll make a great team, the blind leading the blind!"

"Now wait a minute!" Robin feigned an injured look. "I happen to feel *very* confident, and when we get our first Emmy *I* will keep it!" Robin dropped her stack of papers alongside Sally's, then stepped back with raised eyebrows and surveyed her friend. "What's with the blue jeans, Sally? You never dress like that for work."

Sally glanced down at the figure-hugging blue jeans and the bright yellow T-shirt that sported the word HELP! "I felt they fit the occasion. I also wear them for shampooing the dog and giving my car an oil change. I'll be darned if I'm going to ruin any of my TV wardrobe while experimenting in here, Robin." She glanced at Robin's wide-eyed look. "Don't worry, I'll dress nicely for the show. I wouldn't think of embarrassing my producer! But speaking of clothes, look at yourself. I haven't seen you look this ravishing since Robert Redford stopped in for an interview last year. Heavy date?"

"No . . . no, of course not!" Robin's cheeks reddened under Sally's scrutiny. "Well, one never knows when one is going to get stuck in an elevator with P. J. Decker, does one? Who knows, he may miss a turn and walk in *here* by mistake." She grinned impishly. "And he'll mistake *you* for the cleaning lady and wisk *me* off into the sunset!"

Sally laughed in spite of herself. "Well, he better not come in here . . ." She allowed a slight edge to creep into her voice. ". . . or he'll be egged out, and I mean it, Robin! And if the chickens are on my side, they'll be rotten ones!"

Robin's voice grew serious as she faced her friend. "Come on, Sally," she said softly. "We all know how disappointed you are. But you know it isn't P. J. Decker's fault. As a matter of fact, he seems to be a fairly decent person"—she paused and grinned—"in addition to having the sexiest eyes and most beautiful body I've ever seen or hope to see! Relax, Sal. You'll soon be back in the sportscaster's seat and chocolate mousse and cheese soufflé will forever be a thing of the past."

Sally shook her head, a slight flush covering her high cheekbones. Even angry and blue-jean clad, her appearance was striking. She was not "model" pretty, but possessed a type of classic, elegant beauty. Her large eyes were deep and intense, and her nose a perfect complement to her high, carved cheekbones. "Oh, Robin. I know it isn't Decker's fault. But he . . . I . . . oh, let's just drop the subject. Perhaps we just have different tastes in men." She turned quickly, dismissing P. J. Decker from the conversation and her thoughts, and faced the kitchen. "Come on, partner, we have work to do!"

"You're right." Robin grew suddenly businesslike. "I came in earlier today and pulled the recipes you wanted for the first show. All the supplies are in the refrigerator and the cupboard next to it. Why don't you start experimenting with the toffee? It's the easiest. I need to go over this schedule with Mr. Slater so I'll be in the newsroom if you need me. See you later."

"Deserting me already?" Sally moaned.

"Yep. It's all yours, Sally. Shall I bring the crew back for dinner?" Robin teased as she walked toward the door.

"Out!"

Sally pulled a red-checkered apron off a peg and slipped it over her head, tying it tightly around her slender waist. Soon she had the counter covered with sugar, salt, and bowls of assorted shapes and sizes. "Aunt Millie's Toffee" the recipe read. "Oh, Aunt Millie, wherever you are"— Sally cast her eyes upward—"please guide me!" Carefully she heated the cream on a front burner, then added the cream of tartar as the recipe directed. The sizzle of the hot mixture reminded her to mix in the container of sugar at her elbow, which she did in one swift movement. "Maybe this isn't going to be so bad after all," she whispered as she stuck her head into the refrigerator searching for a stick of butter. The combination of sound and smell caused her to pull out of the coolness with a jerk. She was just in time to see hundreds of tiny amber-colored bubbles climbing up over the side of the boiling pan, and moving rapidly onto the stove and floor.

"Sally, let me help." A deep voice filled the small set as a large male form materialized out of the shadows. "You'd be fine if you'd lower your temperature fifteen degrees."

Sally stared into the laughing eyes of Peter Decker. "You . . . you . . ." she sputtered as the brown sticky stream gathered around her feet. "Who are *you,* telling me what to do? *I'm* the cook and you're the sportscaster, remember?" She jerked around and grabbed the steel handle of the boiling pot, then yelped in pain as the heat seared the skin of her palm.

Peter moved quickly toward her, turned on the cold tap water, and held her wrist firmly as he positioned it under the running stream. She tried to pull her hand away, anger and embarrassment filling her eyes. "Let go."

"Shhh," he soothed, gently patting her hand dry while Sally watched, too stunned for the moment to protest. His wide chest touched her shoulders and she found herself acutely aware of the sensuous, musky odor of his after-shave.

Her pulse raced. The heat of the burn was nothing compared to the flaming burning of her rising desire. She was acutely aware of the press of his chest and stomach against her back, the reality of his flesh so close to hers. She closed her eyes for a moment, suddenly weak-kneed and light-headed.

When she looked up again, he was smiling down at her. "Feel better?"

Sally nodded. "What were you doing in here? Spying on me?"

"Nope. Just needed a breath of fresh air. The walls were closing in on me in the newsroom so I prescribed a touch of beauty. Knew it would do the trick. No sabotage intended at all. On my honor." He held his free hand up in an oath, and tightened his hold slightly with the other.

The slight pressure of his hand on her wrist sent a tingling sensation up Sally's arm. The burn was forgotten as her pulse began to race. Hang on, Sally, she warned, hang on. "Well, thank you, Decker. I think it's fine now."

Peter remained immobile, holding her wrist next to his warm body, watching the flicker in her green and violet speckled eyes.

"My hand, Peter. You can return it now." She let her eyes fall into his powerful gaze. "Please?" Her voice sounded tiny when it reached her ears, and she said again in a louder voice, "Please! My hand. It takes two to cook, you know." She forced a faint laugh.

"Yes . . . yes, of course it does," Peter finally answered. "But I think you really ought to abandon the cooking for today. After we bandage this burn you won't want to be near heat for a few hours."

Oh, Sally groaned inwardly, if only you knew. *You* should be what I'm getting away from!

"I'll give you a lift home. It might be difficult for you to manage the steering wheel." He removed several gauze pads from the top drawer of the counter and placed them gently over the reddened area, then wound a light white strip around her hand. "There, we're all set. Let's go." He flicked a switch and the set fell into darkness.

Sally settled back into the soft blue leather of Peter Decker's silver-gray Porsche. This is crazy! Her thoughts crisscrossed through her head. But it *is* quitting time, she rationalized. And I am tired. And it is nice to be driven home. "Peter?" She found her voice. "About my car . . ."

"No problem. I'll have it to your place by morning."

"Do you simply twitch your nose?"

"Something like that." He laughed and looked down at her. "Relax, Sally Denning, and enjoy the ride."

"Well," Sally offered, "it *does* beat cooking."

"You really *don't* like to cook, do you?"

"Decker, I don't know enough about cooking to *know* whether I like it or not! I honestly never cooked, but some people just can't be convinced of that. Bill Slater thinks *every* woman knows how to cook. He believes it's as natural as having babies or primping in a mirror. After my mother died my dad had a wonderful housekeeper come in. She cooked and cleaned and made our beds. And did a terrific job of it. No one ever *wanted* me to cook! On Bertha's days off my brother, Matt, would throw together tuna fish glop and we all loved it. So you see"—she glanced at him sideways—"it's an honest fear that grips me in that little kitchen!"

58

Peter's deep laugh filled the car as they drove down the shady street. "Well, that explains a lot of things—"

"But *you* seemed comfortable in that kitchen," she interrupted, "even knowledgeable."

"Well . . ." Peter sat up straighter in the tiny car and filled his chest with air. "I don't mean to brag, but . . . I *was* known as Delectable Decker when we were on the road." He looked over as Sally tried unsuccessfully to stifle a laugh. "It referred to my *culinary* talents, Miss Denning!" he scolded with laughter in his eyes. "Seriously, one tires pretty quickly of the greasy spoons we find on the road, so I started preparing my own meals. And after five years of it I'm damn good! I've even gone to a couple of New York cooking schools during the winter break. It's great therapy and my teammates loved feasting on fillet of sole à la P. J. and my special curry d'agneau. I even taught some of the wives."

Sally watched him in wonder. This *was* a surprise. His eyes sparkled as he expounded on his gourmet marvels and Sally listened to every word, thoroughly enjoying this new dimension of Peter Decker. Somehow it didn't fit the glamorous, woman-loving image painted by the press, but she was not about to argue that issue now.

"So, my Sally soufflé, if I can be of any help, don't hesitate to call on me." He winked and pulled the car smoothly up to the curb.

Sally's apartment was in a comfortable three-story Victorian home with gingerbread trim and a deep green lawn that stretched down to the street and around to the back. Huge oak trees spread their shade over the budding spring garden edging the wide porch and the freshly painted swing.

Sally waved at several neighborhood boys riding by on their bicycles, then brought her attention back to her companion. "Thanks for the limo service." She paused and fumbled in her purse for her keys. Peter peered in, retrieved them, and dropped them into her open hand. Suddenly Sally was feeling defenseless again. How could she politely avoid inviting him *in*. Yet if she did how would she ever get him *out*. She spoke slowly, stumbling over her words, "Thank you again. I . . . I'd invite you up, but . . ."

"Sally." Peter's voice was low and sensual. He leaned over until his cheek brushed her hair and whispered softly into her ear. "I don't feel rejected, don't worry. I have other plans tonight anyway." Sally jerked upright as he unfolded his legs from behind the steering wheel, moved out and around the front of the car, and held open Sally's door. His expression was calm and unreadable, but beneath hooded lids his eyes were filled with amusement. Sally stepped from the car and walked stiffly toward the house, wondering why *she* suddenly felt like the rejected party.

As she walked into the studio on Monday morning Sally willed herself to be calm. Robin's face beamed with excitement. "You look marvelous, Sally! We'll wow 'em!"

Sally smiled, trying to borrow some of Robin's enthusiasm for her demeanor as she walked up on the set. Ten minutes to zero hour! She smoothed her soft, silky skirt and straightened the neckline on her emerald-green blouse. Her hair glowed as the lights reflected off the golden surface and the flush in her cheeks set off the hazel sparkle in her eyes. She stood behind the butcher-block counter, checked her utensils, and smiled at the cameraman. She was ready. This was it! A hush settled over the studio.

Suddenly Sally was aware of a sharp, dangerous prickling behind her eyelids and across the bridge of her nose. Oh, no. She panicked, pinching the bridge of her nose with two fingers and holding her breath. She darted a glance at the cueman hovering silently at stage left, at Robin's ear-phoned silhouette in the control room, and then up to the clock. Five seconds . . . four . . . three. As the digital numbers slid to zero, Sally released her breath, rested her trembling hands on the counter before her, smiled into the camera—and sneezed.

A groan echoed through the studio. Sally blushed furiously, the blood rising past the collar of her shirt to her ears and cheeks. Her eyes watered. She wished she could drop out of sight, crawl into the microwave, anything to disappear. Instead, she whispered a shaky "thank you" to the cueman's muttered "bless you," forced a bright, winning smile, and introduced the unseen audience to her first show.

By the time Sally began preparing chicken almondine, she was feeling much more comfortable, carried by the excitement of being in front of the camera's eye. Cheeks flushed, pulse quickened. The strain faded from her smile and she sparkled with the confidence and good humor that had previously won her so many loyal viewers. So what if all the almonds weren't sliced into neat, smooth little slivers? She gave the errant ones a few hasty hacks with her cleaver and hurried on with a grin and some unrehearsed patter. "A good cook is always aware of the importance of timing. Each ingredient must be added at just the right moment. See how our butter is bubbling in the pan. I *think* that has something to do with 'clarifying' butter. But, umm . . . we'll clarify that point on our next show." A loud guffaw broke from the cueman as he immediately tossed his stack of prepared cards on the floor.

And moments later, when the first wet, slippery chicken breast slipped from her fingers onto the polished floor, she didn't miss a beat. Still smiling into the camera, she bent down and retrieved it. She explained to her audience: "Should your breast land on the floor, simply give it a good washing off, toss a little more seasoning on it—like that—and proceed!"

Nothing deterred her. Not seeing Robin slumped with her head buried in her hands. Not the silly grin on the cameraman's face. Not the slightly charred edges of her toasted almonds. When the chicken stuck stubbornly to the pan, resisting her restrained on-camera attempts to dislodge it, she simply turned her back to the camera. This wiped the smile off the cameraman's face and sent him scurrying after a new angle. While the audience was being treated to a wild panned shot of the walls and cabinets, Sally speared the chicken mercilessly with her spatula handle. She turned back and slid the offending morsels onto the waiting plates.

Ten seconds before the camera's red eye blinked shut, Sally smiled confidently into it, held the platters aloft for the audience's perusal, and cheerfully pronounced her closing lines: "This is Sally Denning, thanking you for joining me. And I'll see you next week on *The Back Burner*."

She paused five seconds, then whispered through a fixed smile without moving her lips, "Are we off the air yet?" The cameraman nodded. Sally took a deep breath, pushed back her shoulders, and shouted, "Help!" In one bound Robin was out of the control room and at her friend's side.

"We did it! Not bad, Sally!"

Sally shook her head in disbelief. "Good grief, do I always have to be teamed with the eternal optimist?" She gave the younger girl an affectionate squeeze, then headed out of the studio with Robin close behind, thanking the studio crew along her way. A now familiar form was leaning against the door. As Sally approached, Peter broke into smiles and applauded.

"Nice job, Sally. The show looked good."

"Were you here the whole time?"

"From sneeze to finish!"

Sally groaned. "Oh, Decker." Turning away, she headed for the newsroom. Peter caught up with her and matched her step. "Really, Sally, I may have seen better cooking in my day, but I've never seen a cook with more charm and personality! I can't speak for the chicken, but *you* were delicious!"

Sally was still blushing as she pushed open the doors to the newsroom. Beaver jumped up and flashed the V-for-victory sign. "Way to go, Sally. The show looked good. As a matter of fact"—he laughed—"I've never enjoyed a cooking show more!" Bill Slater came to the door of his office, holding his phone.

"Sally! This phone call was for you. It was Adelle Williams."

Sally flinched, but Slater continued, a grin creasing his face. "Our esteemed owner just called to tell you she enjoyed your show. Seems she and her friends found you to be a delightful combination of Julia Child and Jerry Lewis! They can't wait until next week's show!"

The room dissolved into laughter. Sally faced them. "Okay, folks, you laugh! But what none of you realize is that I have just cooked the only two things in my entire repertoire! And as soon as I finish the day's work"—she tossed her head—"I am going home to soak and sulk!"

After the disastrous events of the day, it felt good to be alone in her apartment. Sally let her clothes fall in a heap on the floor and lowered herself wearily into the hot, sweet-scented bubbles floating in her bath. The water rose over the tight knot in her stomach, the aching hollow of her chest, the tense muscles of her shoulders and neck. Leaning her head back against the tub's smooth rim, she closed her eyes. Immediately a hundred confused images flashed before her—her face crumpled in a sneeze on the monitor, boiling pots, slippery chicken, Beaver's grin, Robin's giggles, Slater's cigar, and Decker's brown eyes filled with encouragement.

"Damn! Can't a woman have a little privacy in her own bathroom!" she complained loudly to the empty apartment. Climbing out of the tub, she wrapped a towel around her slim frame and tucked the ends into the valley between her breasts. Wet footsteps marked her path into the kitchen. Reaching into a cupboard, she lifted down an ornate decanter and one tiny cut-crystal sherry glass. "For medicinal purposes only," she muttered, and took a tentative sip of the rich golden liquid. "Ummm—not bad, not bad at all."

Back in the bathroom she dropped the towel next to her discarded clothes, balanced the glass on the flat top of the soap holder, and sank back into the water. "Definitely better!" By the time she emptied her second glass, Sally was feeling a lot better. She could even laugh at the thought of her ill-timed sneeze. As a matter of fact, it was very, very funny! The laughter swelled within her, shaking her shoulders, filling her. "Oops, was that the phone?" She stifled her laughter and listened. "Nope, the doorbell. Well, too bad." She leaned back and sank beneath the water until only her head and knees were showing. The water tickled her ears and cheeks and her hair floated like a halo around her face. As soon as she sat up the ringing of the doorbell resumed. "Oh, no, not now! Go away!" she called. "No one is home." The bell chimed again, insistent, demanding. "Okay, okay, I'm coming." She stepped out of the tub, toweled off, and grabbed the robe hanging on a hook behind the door. She tied the sash in a knot around her narrow waist and without a glance in the mirror padded across the living room and pulled the door open.

"No! Tell me I'm seeing things."

"What vision fair doth greet thine eyes?" his deep voice answered.

"I was thinking more along the lines of nightmare."

"Does that mean you're *not* happy to see me?" Pete Decker stood in the doorway, clad in an enormous black raincoat, his good arm straining to maintain its grip on two bulging grocery sacks. A forest-green stalk of broccoli poked its flowery head from one bag; a carton of eggs teetered precariously atop the other.

"Well?" he asked, his sweat-dotted brows lifting questioningly. "What do you think?"

"I think you're crazy! What are you doing here?"

"I've just climbed three very long flights of stairs to give you your first cooking lesson," he panted. "Think we could continue this conversation inside?"

Sally laughed softly and grabbed one of the sacks. "Come on."

He followed behind her into the tiny kitchen and dropped his burden next to hers on the Formica counter top. "Ah, thank you, kind lady." He turned, stepped close, and rested his chin on her shoulder. "I think I've lost all feeling in my arms."

His cheek was but an inch from hers, the weight of his chin poking playfully into her shoulder. She was intensely aware of the heat of his body next to hers and the slight tang of his sweat mixed with the subtle scent of his after-shave.

"Mmm, smells good!"

He had read her thoughts. Then the sensuous look from under his half-closed lids told her he was talking about her. In a flash she realized she was standing in the middle of her kitchen, clad only in a bathrobe, back in Pete Decker's arms.

"Oh, no, you don't! If you're here to practice your sweet talk—"

"Wait!" He laughed, his hands spread open in the air between them. "No, honestly. You just seem to have that effect on me. I'm here on a noble mission. *Voilà!*" With a gesture worthy of a stage-bound Dracula, he swung wide his raincoat, revealing his muscular body wrapped in an apron. Stenciled in red block letters across its front were the words, Kiss the Cook.

"I will not!" Sally warned, taking a step backward.

"Ahhh, so much for advertising." He winked and that boyish-innocent smile that she would always associate only with him spread across his face. "I'll take a rain check." He shrugged, his shoulders rolling beneath the thin cloth of his blue cotton shirt. "But now it's time to get down to business." He unbuttoned his cuffs and began to roll his sleeves to the elbow.

Then he stopped. His eyes darkened strangely. The temperature in the tiny kitchen seemed to soar. Sally could feel a prickling, liquid sensation wash over her limbs, circle round her knees. She took an unplanned step backward, steadying herself with one hand on the counter top. Peter leaned forward into the space where her body had been. So close now. His eyes traveled lingeringly over the outline of her body beneath the thin robe.

"First I've got to ask a favor. A man can only take so much. And I've never been known for my restraint! If you stand here in that flimsy little thing for one more moment . . ." He reached out and fingered the silky fabric of her robe. She could feel the material slide over her still damp skin. The backs of his fingers brushed her flesh. She was melting, melting . . . "One more moment," he continued, mischief and desire glinting in his narrowed eyes, "and I won't be responsible for my actions. Maybe you'd better change into something else."

With mischief masking the shakiness she felt inside, Sally asked, "And what exactly, sir, would you like me to change into, a frog or a princess?"

With a swat on her well-shaped bottom, he banished her to the bedroom.

She stopped short when she caught a glimpse of her reflection in the mirrored closet doors. *This* was how she looked to P.J. Decker? Quickly she brushed out her hair, feathering the damp tendrils away from her face. She slipped into a pair of comfortable jeans and a loose middy blouse. Not satisfied, she pulled off her shirt and replaced it with a form-hugging cotton-knit sweater, its deep plum color a rich background for her fair coloring. She applied a touch of color to her cheeks and lips, a hint of darkness to her lashes. "There!" she said, with a pleased smile at the woman in the mirror.

When she stepped back into the kitchen, Pete's approving glance told her she had made the right choice.

"Today we are going to prepare a springtime feast," he announced in a professorial voice. "Your viewers will love you." He pointed to the first stack of groceries. "This is going to be your appetizer, Spring Fever Spaghettini."

Sally looked quickly at the display of fresh vegetables—bright red pepper, emerald zucchini, fuzzy dill, and dark orange carrots. She nodded as his pointing finger shifted to the next group. "This next is your entree—grilled salmon with tarragon. I can taste it now. Yummy! Someday I'll take you down to Pat's; that's a little fish store down in Kansas City that flies everything in fresh daily. You'll love it!" His brows jumped together. "How do you feel about blue?" Her answering shrug did nothing to deter his enthusiasm. "That's okay, we'll give it a try."

"And this"—he pointed to the smallest of the piles—"this is the pièce de résistance! Almond tulips with fresh raspberry ice. All pink and white. Isn't that romantic?"

She looked up with soulful eyes. "Pete? The only kind of ice I know how to make is the kind that pops out of my freezer trays."

"No problem, Sally. It's really easy. Really." He wrapped his arms round her shoulders, laughing. "That's what's so much fun. It only looks hard, but it's easy and delicious. Kind of like falling in love."

Sally shook her head and pushed a hand against his chest. She could feel his heart beating under her palm. "You are the craziest man I've ever met, Peter Decker." She meant to scold but it didn't come out that way.

He smiled at her in pleasure. "Ah, well, falling in love

67

will have to wait. First things first. I'll need a garlic press, a wisk, a large saucepan, copper-bottomed preferably, your food processor, and— Have I said something wrong?"

Sally was doubled up against the refrigerator door, her shoulders shaking with laughter. ". . . a garlic press . . . a . . . a . . . copper-bottomed . . ." She gasped between peals of laughter.

Decker stood with his hands on his hips, watching her, his mouth twitching slightly in a repressed smile. "And what is so funny about that?"

"Decker, you really didn't believe me. I *don't* cook. Here, look." She pointed at the old four-burner stove. "Only one burner works. The others gave up the ghost long ago. And here"—she pulled open a ceramic-knobbed drawer to reveal a neat, but skimpy, array of knives, forks, and spoons—"*no* garlic press, *no* whisk. I'm lucky I've got a peeler to peel your carrots!"

"You *don't* peel them. You scrub them!"

His mock seriousness sent Sally into renewed gales of laughter. "Oh, Decker. What do you do with your zucchini?"

She sank to the floor holding her aching sides and Peter dropped down beside her, his rich laughter filling the small apartment. As their laughter subsided into chuckles, the chuckles into easy smiles, Pete leaned across and kissed her—once—on the tip of her nose.

"I haven't laughed like that in years, Sally. Thank you."

She shook her head, feeling suddenly shy. "Neither have I. It was nice."

"Very." They sat for another moment, then Pete started to rise. He winced and sat back, rubbing his strapped shoulder. "Ow! Darn thing! Keeps reminding me when I don't want to be reminded."

"Reminds you of what?"

He looked at her for a moment before answering. "I

don't know, Sally. My own weakness . . . the whims of fortune . . ." His gaze held hers and she was filled with a sudden burning desire to open her heart to him, to share her own vulnerability. She wanted to tell him about the confusion he'd made her feel but hesitated, her long-held reserve inhibiting her. The moment passed.

Decker smiled softly and rose to his feet. "Come on." He offered his hand and helped her up. "Let's go find somewhere else to practice."

"The studio?" she asked, hoping and not hoping.

"No. It's late now. Let's go to my place." He studied her face. "All right?"

"Sure," she answered as casually as possible. "Let me help you put all of this back together."

They carried the bags of groceries back through the living room. Sally flicked off the lights, then closed the door behind them.

Decker led the way down the stairs and out onto the street. He came to a halt beside his low, sleek Porsche. Sally shifted her package, waiting for P. J. to locate his keys.

As her neighbors Mr. and Mrs. McCuller hurried by, they did a double take, stopped, and eyed the young couple. "Well, good evening, Sally. Out for a night on the town?"

"Evening, George, Helen." Sally smiled.

"Is that young feller there P. J. Decker?"

Peter smiled across the roof of the car. "Evening, sir."

"Well I'll be. Hey, Ralph!"

An older man sitting on the stoop looked up.

"Look who's here. It's P. J. Decker, with Sally!" Sally ducked down behind the grocery sack. Just then a dog ran up, barking loudly, and stopped to sniff around the package. Two boys followed close on his heels.

"Hey, P. J. Decker," the first hissed.

"Yeah, you're right, Tony!" The second grinned. "Hey, P. J. How ya doing?"

"Fine thanks, fellows." P. J. smiled. "And you?"

The two nodded happily and stood there, kicking at the ground with the already scuffed toes of their sneakers.

Sally glared at Decker, silently urging him to hurry. And as if on cue, he tugged the keys loose from his pocket and waved them in the air. With a flip of his wrist the door opened. He stashed the packages in the rear well, helped Sally into the low-slung front seat, and got in beside her. With a wave at the assembled group on the sidewalk, they were off.

"Whew! Thought for a moment I'd lost the keys."

"How did you manage to get them into your back pocket with your bad arm anyway?" she snapped.

Peter took his eyes from the road and looked at her. "Sally? What are you mad about now?"

"Nothing." There were two spots of color high on her cheekbones. "I just don't like making a scene."

"For a girl who doesn't like being in the public eye, I'd say you sure picked the wrong business." He was watching the road again. Sally could see the muscles jumping along his jaw.

"That's not the same thing!" she insisted, her voice rising. "That's my *job*. But my life is my own."

"Some of us aren't that lucky." His knuckles were white against the steering wheel as he drove on. When they stopped at a red light he turned toward her. "Listen, I'm sorry if that embarrassed you, but that's who I am. My 'job' isn't quite that cut and dry. I can't switch off the TV set, or walk away from the mike, and have it all end. People know me, recognize me. They want something."

"And you've got to give it to them?"

"Sometimes, yes"—he nodded—"if they don't want too much. If it doesn't hurt anyone. It's the price I pay for doing what I love—and being good at it. And the two minutes it takes to give some kid an autograph, or be nice to those two boys back there, hell, that means something! You know, I can remember waiting in line to get Hank Aaron's autograph on my first glove." His voice softened. "I've still got that glove, Sally. And here I am with a chance to be like that. To be somebody's hero. It's a part of who I am, and what I do and the fact that I do it damn well. Although you'd never know it now, would you, Sally? God, how I miss the feel of that ball in my hand, the sound of the fans."

"Oh, Peter," Sally whispered, reaching out to touch his arm. "I hadn't thought of how difficult this must be for you."

He shrugged out from under her hand. "No. Don't be nice now, please."

They drove the last thirty miles in silence, broken only by scattered comments on the weather, or a herd of sheep, or an especially lovely farm glimpsed through a window. The rest of the time neither spoke, lost in their own thoughts. Pete drove the back roads, avoiding the highway. As they approached Kansas City, he turned off onto a small county road. Soon their way was blocked by a brick gatehouse. Sally recognized the entrance to Lake Winnepeg, a very private, prestigious group of homes built on the wooded hills surrounding a lovely lake. She had been there once before, to a boating picnic, and remembered her amazement at finding this lovely spot on the edge of the city.

At that moment a uniformed guard stepped from the shadowed interior. He peered down into the car, then smiled and straightened, touching his hand to his cap in salute. "Evening, Mr. Decker, sir."

"Evening, Ross." With a wave, Pete gunned the car through the gate and up the long, winding drive.

"I'm surprised he didn't fire off the twenty-one guns," Sally commented, sarcasm coating her words.

Peter stepped on the brake and pulled the car to the edge of the road. "Okay, that's it! Sally, you're impossible. You don't like the crowds, the adulation, the notoriety, and now you don't like what it takes to keep all that at bay. I live here because it affords me a little privacy. A place to be myself, by myself." He paused and looked at her closely, his eyes dark and depthless. "Tell me, is there anything you *do* like about my life?"

"You," Sally answered, her heart melting into her stomach.

"Ah," Pete said and smiled. "You do have a way with words, lady." He nodded. "That was nice."

"But I thought I wasn't supposed to be nice."

"It's okay, I can stand nice now." He continued driving through the darkening hills and parked in front of a sprawling, stone ranch. "Home."

Sally let her eyes drift over the rambling house with the beautiful stone facade and the lovely stained-glass panel over the front door. "Wow!" She whistled, but caught his look. "Nice," she said. "Nice."

The rooms inside were all that the outside had promised. They were beautifully decorated and each one opened onto either an inner courtyard or a wide expanse of redwood deck. From every window there was a sweeping panorama of the surrounding hills and the lake below.

"Very nice, Decker. I approve."

"I was hoping you would. That there's the dining room, over there the library, this is the so-called family room"— he grinned—"not much used as yet. And this"—he led her on toward the back of the house—"this is *my* kitchen."

The room was enormous, with a butcher block island in the center that housed the stove top as well as a little eating area. "Just right for two." He smiled. Sally took a tour while P. J. unpacked. In an addition off the main room she found a garbage disposal, dishwasher, and a temperature-controlled wine cellar. At the other end was a wet bar, a tiny refrigerator filled with lemons, limes, coconut milk, and cherries, and a lovely built-in glass and liquor cabinet. The central area was reserved, as Johnny cheerfully told her, for serious business! He had already restacked the groceries and collected his cooking tools, lined like gleaming surgical instruments along the edge of the island.

"Now this is what I call cooking." Peter looked as happy as a clam at high tide. In a matter of minutes he was wisking cream, parmesan, and spices for his spaghettini, pressing garlic and mincing chives for the salmon, and had Sally "frothing" egg whites for raspberry ice. He did it all with running commentary and they joked and laughed. After one particularly flat joke, Sally sent a spoonful of egg whites flying across the counter top. It landed square on his cheek. With a chuckle Pete stuck out his tongue, licked the little dollop, and pronounced her a master chef.

She stood across the island from him, the three feet of counter top a perfect distance for observing, and being observed. Time and again she looked up from her stirring to find his eyes on her face studying her brow, her nose, the line of her chin. She thrilled at the delight in his eyes, found herself smiling, humming softly. The recipe was suddenly manageable; batter became tulip shells, pale pink ice hardened in the freezer. She watched him slice julienne vegetables, and when he looked up and found her staring, he offered her the knife.

"Come here. I'll show you how."

Peter stood behind her, his chest and hips pressed ever so pleasantly against her back, and held his hand over hers to demonstrate the correct technique. Sally, her concentration divided, knew it was sheer luck that kept her from slicing a fingertip into the perfectly pared produce.

73

"Am I doing this right?" she asked, just to hear his voice.

"Better than right, perfect. You know what?" His voice purred.

"Hmmm?"

"You are beautiful, Sally." He leaned his cheek against hers. "Really, so beautiful. I can't seem to keep my eyes off you."

"Nor your hands." Sally turned her face and kissed his cheek. The shadow of his beard set her lips tingling, but his skin was cool, fresh, and sweet.

His hand cupped her head, his fingers brushing her cheek. He kissed her, a sweet, lingering kiss, his lips grazing across hers. Then he sprinkled a shower of light, playful kisses across her face, his lips a feather's touch on her eyelids and cheeks. "You taste so good, much better than salmon tarragon, I'd say." He burrowed his face into her nape, his warm breath sending shivers of arousal spreading across her skin.

"Oh, no, you don't! You promised me a *cooking* lesson." She turned to face him within the tiny space left between the curve of his body and the counter top. Her movement brought every inch of her body in contact with his, his warmth flowing into her breasts, hips, thighs. A sudden throbbing in the secret center of her being began, urgent, and hungering. She struggled to quell its beat, repeating teasingly, "Come on, Pete, hadn't we better get back to our vegetables while they're still . . . crisp?"

His lips parted slightly and she could see the white, even edge of his teeth. "Don't worry, Sally. I'm a man of honor. A promise is a promise, but we have a minute. Things are simmering nicely."

"Coming to a boil, I'd say." With uncharacteristic brazenness she slipped one hand behind the open collar of his shirt. His body was so warm, so alive and sensual under her fingertips. A smile curved his lips.

74

He lifted his arms and gently, slowly, moved his hands down over the curves of her body. His caressing palms found the fullness of her breasts, the tuck of her waist, the gentle swell of her hips, the flatness of her belly. His touch thrilled her, filled her with light-headed giddiness. "Soup's on!" She laughed nervously. She waited the span of ten pounding heartbeats. "Pete, you wouldn't send me out onto that set with half-a-salmon show now, would you?"

He laughed with her, a strange huskiness in his voice. "Okay, angel, recess is over. It's back to class. But let me tell you"—he brushed the damp hair back from his forehead—"the cook was about ready to throw in his apron." With a light kiss, more of a promise than a touch, he moved back around to his side of the counter.

Pretending her full attention was focused on his instructions, Sally watched him. Watched his hands, his face, his eyes. Every movement, every expression, every look delighted her. He was gentle, soft-spoken, caring, sensitive— the exact opposite of the picture painted by the media. Yet he was still "P. J." Decker. There was no mistaking that ease and confidence, the perfect proportions of his body, the aura of sensuality that surrounded him.

Watch your step, Sal, she cautioned herself. It would be easy, too easy, to lose yourself to this man. After all this time, all this pride, and to what avail? It would never work. Her thoughts were interrupted by his touch on her arm.

"There. All finished. What do you think?"

Sally eyed the beautifully garnished platters. "Peter, did we do that?" She chuckled. "It's so gorgeous it almost looks too good to eat!"

"Good. Now for the final touches. This is just for you and me, okay?"

She smiled and helped him set the table in the dining room. Soon candles threw glimmering shadows off the walls, hand-thrown stoneware decorated the dark oak table, and chilled white wine sparkled in pewter goblets.

"The proof of the pudding." He grinned, pushing in her chair. He sat across from her, the candlelight locking them in its intimate circle.

"To Lady Luck. And to you, my lady." He lifted his glass, touched hers, and sipped.

Sally drank the dry, sparkling wine, mingling its taste with the richly spiced taste of the pasta, the tangy flavor of the salad, the melt-in-your-mouth taste of the salmon. It was late now, the undraped windows darkened by night's own curtain. The late April breeze blowing in from the lake carried a hint of rain and the candlelight flickered.

Pete rose from his seat and came to stand behind Sally. He draped his arms around her shoulders and leaned his face against her hair. "Shall I light the fire? We could take your raspberry romance and the brandy out into the library. Sound good?"

"Sounds like heaven," Sally murmured. They carried dessert into the cozy wood-paneled library. A beautifully patterned Navaho rug decorated the wood floors and at the far end, in front of the hearth, there were two butter-leather love seats. Sally sank onto one, tucking her legs beneath her and balancing the brandy snifters on her knees.

Pete knelt before her on the hearth laying the fire. Soon sparks crackled among the kindling and Peter expertly fed the fuel until the flames were blue and crimson ribbons waving in the chimney's draught.

He rolled back on his heels and sat staring into the flames.

Sally stared only at him. There in the firelight he looked more like a sculpture than a man. The marblelike smoothness of his flesh, the coil of muscle beneath the skin. Temptation overtook her and she placed the brandy on the table, leaned over, and laid her hand on his good shoulder.

She stroked her palm down his back and felt his muscles twitch beneath her fingertips.

When he looked up, it was with a face she had never seen before. His eyes were glazed with desire, a light beading of sweat dotting his brow. He reached up, took hold of her arm, and pulled her down onto his lap. The room spun around them as they tumbled backward onto the rough surface of the rug.

"Umph . . ." Pete grunted in pain as his shoulder struck the floor.

"Oh, Pete. I'm sorry!" Sally breathed through the thick fog of her desire. "Did I hurt . . ."

"Forget it!" he rasped, holding her tightly against him. Their bodies were molded together, length to length. He brushed the frown from her brow. "Forget it, angel. That's not what I want you thinking about now."

She kissed his chin and looked up. "And what *do* you want me thinking about?"

"Me. Only me. About how good I feel here next to you. The touch of my hands . . ." He slid his hands beneath the sweater's mesh and cupped the swelling sides of her breasts. ". . . the taste of my lips . . ." He kissed her breath away.

Again the room spun, the floor was tilting beneath her and the ceiling swirling. There was nothing real, nothing to hold on to but Peter. She tightened her arms around his neck. Her hips stirred, beginning the sweet dance of desire.

The kiss lasted for eternity . . . and was over too soon. It was better than chocolates and Sally was hungry for more.

What's happening to me? Remember who this man is! The caution blew across her brain and vanished like a puff of smoke. Her common sense had deserted her; her usual reserve evaporated in the sudden heat of her yearning. She sought his mouth again.

"Sally," he moaned beneath her lips. "Sally, I want you."

She heard the urgency in his voice and her body answered of its own accord. Fires were ignited deep within her; flames licked their fiery tongues up and down her spine. Her body was taut with anticipation, fluid and throbbing. With trembling fingers she unbuttoned his shirt and spread it open. His tanned chest gleamed in the firelight. His bronze body, covered with sandy hair, was warm and rough to her touch. She lowered her face and kissed his chest, her hands drawing patterns of pleasure on his skin.

"Sally . . . Sally . . ." Her name was a prayer and a curse on his lips. His body moved against hers, hard with desire. His hands fondled her breasts, the thumbs rotating over the pink circles of delicate flesh at their tips. His lips descended to follow in the fiery path of his fingertips, and Sally arched her back, lifted her mouth from his skin, and drew a long, shuddering sigh.

Peter's hands stroked her back and buttocks. His urgent fingers unzipped her jeans, then his own, removing the last restraint.

In searing heat their bodies met and melted together.

"Peter, hold me. Tighter, tighter."

His hands reached for her, gathering her to him. His desire rode him like a master.

Sally ran her fingers down his chest, across his abdomen. She felt the muscles convulse under her palms. Rough hair. Smooth skin. Heat and motion. Then his fingers traveled the length of her body, touching and not touching . . . tantalizing, teasing, teaching.

"I want to know you, Sally, every inch of you. I want to touch you, taste you." Shifting his weight, he moved his head down across her breasts. His mouth was warm and hungry on her nipples, the tender ridge of her ribs. She felt his thick hair brushing the underside of her breasts, his cool cheek resting against the feverish, quivering skin of her stomach. His tongue rasped back and forth across her flesh, setting the taut fibers of her nerves thrumming like the strings of a finely tuned violin.

"Pete, I need you. I want to know you too."

Her excitement fluttered in her throat. Reaching down, she tangled her fingers in his sandy hair, felt his head turn beneath her palms as his mouth grazed hungrily across her body.

Her hands began again to stroke and to caress him, flowing across his back and hips. She curled, shifted, straining to reach and fondle previously untouched places . . . slid down under him until once again they were pressed length to length . . . molded together, melted together. Her hands sought his loins, the hard curve of his hips and buttocks.

Soft love words escaped her lips . . . and she heard him whisper her name in a fever of excitement. Then his hands —guiding, urging—slid beneath her, lifting her . . . and he was there, his desire barely held in check . . . as he waited, waited for her to welcome him . . . and she drew him to her.

Sally felt the wild, rising surge of him within her—and a wild, exultant freedom. The world fell away. It was this surprising, treasured man . . . and her. Alone. The two of them. Surrounded by a circling, sweeping sea. A whirlpool of sensations and delight spinning her . . . and him. Alone. The two of them, caught and clinging to each other in a wild and joyous vortex that surged deeper, deeper—drawing her to the sweet, secret center of all being . . . deeper, deeper . . . he filled her, every fiber, every hollow . . . and she felt building within her, unstoppable, a rippling . . . rippling . . . the sea filling her, each fiber flooded with fulfilled desire.

And as if the tide turned, it carried them, still enmeshed in each other's arms, to the waiting shore of the rough

79

Navaho rug. Sally lay pressed against Pete's good side, her cheek against his warm shoulder. His fingers brushed her face, and with his thumb he traced the curve of her cheek, like a sculptor memorizing the lines of a cherished work of art. She reached up and entwined her slender fingers with his.

"I like your body," she whispered.

"That makes us even, then, my sweet Sally. For I like yours . . ."

Sally rubbed her flushed cheek against his warm flesh. "You are so surprising to me. I get all my feelings neatly aligned . . . and here you come, wreaking havoc."

Pete leaned up on his good arm to study her face with his dark eyes. His voice was deep and rough. "Aligned against me, Sally?"

She smiled ruefully, her eyes meeting and holding his. "Perhaps. But you wouldn't send a rookie onto the field without some line of defense, would you? Aside from the fact that this is *not* my game . . . I have the distinct feeling I'm in the wrong league!"

"No, Sally!" He caught her fingertips between his teeth and nibbled. "Sally, don't worry . . ."

"But I must, Decker! I've got a lot to lose."

"Will you at least stay the night?"

She rubbed her palms against the warm, rough fur of his chest. "I think not, Decker. My own bed sounds a lot safer . . . even if a lot colder."

CHAPTER FOUR

Sally smoothed her softly pleated skirt and sat staring at the shiny silver bowls lining the countertop. She fingered a wooden spoon, dropped it in a bowl, and glanced at the clock. Ten minutes after nine. Robin was late. Where could she be? Didn't she know they had a show to plan?! Sally stood and paced around the small set, then reached for a cookbook and flipped disinterestedly through several pages.

"Slow down, Sally," The deep, husky voice jarred her. Yet she had been expecting it. Waiting for it. Dreading it. "Are you just going to look at the pictures? Don't tell me my devoted and tireless teaching efforts were wasted . . ." His words lingered in the space between them and Sally felt her temperature rise.

She turned and faced him, calming herself and feigning a brightness that belied her sleepless night. "Of course they weren't wasted, Decker. It's simply a matter of the apprentice unable to keep up with the master . . ." After that they'd been so close. She hated speaking in doubletalk, and wished she could voice her true feelings, her fears of getting too involved and with someone who led a

81

life she knew she could never fit into . . . nor wanted to. But she couldn't begin to explain that—not to P.J. Decker —not to a superstar who had had more women than he could count, who had no reason to think in terms of commitment . . . or stable life patterns.

"Sally—" Pete was next to her now, his breath warming her skin. His fingers traced a wavy pattern down the side of her cheek. Sally shivered, then backed away and sought the refuge of a tall stool behind the counter. Pete watched her quietly, then his face grew serious. "Sally, it was beautiful last night. . . ." His words rose, seeking a response.

Sally avoided his eyes when she answered. "Yes . . . Decker. That it was. One beautiful night." She tried to laugh lightly. "I guess I never did get around to thank you for the cooking lesson."

"My pleasure, Sally." His eyes twinkled and Sally wished fervently that Robin would burst through the doors. "But you gave me plenty in return—"

Her brows shot up. In return? Did he consider their lovemaking payment? No, of course he didn't. She knew enough about Pete Decker to know he wasn't callous. She was grasping at straws, that's all. An excuse to be angry and shove him out of her life.

"Sally, how about dinner tonight? Perhaps another cooking lesson . . ."

"No!" Pete was startled at the intensity of her response. "I mean, no, Decker. I—I have other plans for dinner tonight," she lied.

Pete's brows furrowed as he tried to understand. "Sally, what is it? I . . . well, I know you enjoyed last night as much as I did. And I enjoy *you*, Sal—I'd like to get to know you better."

"P.J." Sally kept her voice low and controlled. "I like you too." Her body stiffened as Pete reached out and touched her hand. She quickly removed it from the countertop. "But I don't think . . . I don't want to see you again." There. It was out. I don't want to have dinner with you, Pete Decker, because I can't seem to control my feelings about you—because I could just possibly fall in love with you, and we both know how impossible that would be.

Pete Decker watched her closely, this lithesome beauty who had touched something inside of him—a place no other woman had ever come near—and he tried to read between her words. At last he smiled softly. "Well, Sally, I have time. I'll be patient—for a while. And I'll be here, no matter what you say. I won't give up, my Sally soufflé —you'll see."

And he was gone, leaving Sally feeling dejected and lonely and questioning her sanity again . . . and again . . . and again.

In the weeks that followed, spring came in all its glory to the small Kansas town, intoxicating the townsfolk and students as they exuberantly shed their winter gloom. Thick oaks and maples canopied the quiet streets, and flowers opened wide blooms in colorful window boxes.

Sally had tried painfully to avoid Pete. Their relationship was impossible—and the sooner they *both* realized it, the better. Her common sense told her it was all wasted emotion. Then why did she feel so desolate?

Plucking a purple pansy from the garden, Sally meandered down the old brick walkway in front of her apartment house. She gazed at the flower's soft petals and gingerly touched the velvet surface with her finger. "You're a beautiful pansy, open and lovely," she mused. "And me? I'm just a pansy!" She tucked the flower into a buttonhole in her bright yellow blouse and kicked at a stone in frustration. What has happened to me? she thought in helpless confusion. Where did that Sally Denning go whom I knew so well? The one who avoided hopeless situations like the plague and always knew exactly what she wanted and how to get it? Something *had* changed within Sally. Something deep in the hidden parts of herself had changed and Sally knew it. But she didn't know what to do about it.

Keeping Peter Decker at bay was proving most difficult. His warm smile and dark, coaxing eyes were constantly focused on her, setting her limbs tingling and her heart pounding. His nearness held her captive when they passed in the hall. The curve of his lips embraced her from afar. Each time he would come to lean on her desk or linger at the studio door with invitations and enticements she felt her emotions slip back into his embrace. She remembered the overwhelming loveliness of his body enmeshed with hers and the tenderness of their lovemaking.

It all frightened Sally. Some days she'd cloak herself in humor. Other days she'd pull anger about her for protection—anger at Pete's power over her, anger over losing her job, anger that he had dropped into her life and would just as abruptly drop out of it again. And most of all, anger that she thought of him every morning and every night.

Sally slid into her convertible, turned the ignition, and sped down the sleepy street toward work, scattering squirrels and the newspapers that had missed their early-morning mark.

"Hey, Sally, don't forget the meeting at ten in Slater's office." Robin skidded to a stop as she and Sally met in front of the cooking set door.

"Meeting?"

Robin shook her head. "Sal, how can you manage to do such a terrific job here at the studio and yet seem a thousand miles away? You've got me worried. What are you thinking about?"

Sally shrugged, offering only a smile as answer. She and *The Back Burner* had been a success. By applying her clear thinking to cooking instruction and adding a dash of humor, she had won herself an appreciative viewing audience. Sally steered clear of spaghettini and salmon and concentrated on chicken breasts and steamed vegetables, teaching both herself and the many cooks at home the basics before they tackled gourmet delicacies.

Sally's soft laugh filtered through the hallway in front of set three. "Don't know, Robin. I think it's genetic. I come from a long line of deep thinkers. Now, about this meeting, I'm supposed to come?"

"Yes, my friend," Robin explained patiently. "It's to iron out the details about the annual meeting at the Ozarks this weekend."

"Oh!" Sally's hand flew to her mouth. "That's right! And I *did* forget. I had planned on driving down and spending a couple of days with my dad. I missed last weekend."

"Well, listen, don't worry. Isn't his nursing home down that way?"

"Yes," Sally answered thoughtfully. "Yes, it is. I guess I could stop on the way back. At least we'd have a few hours together. I really miss him, Robin, and my visits mean so much to him."

"I know they do, Sal. I thought maybe that's where you were this past weekend. We missed you at the Staffords' party."

"Oh, well, I . . ." Sally groped for a ready excuse. She had purposely avoided both the nursing home and the party, troubled by her ambivalent feelings over Peter Decker and her life at the moment. "Did . . . was everyone there?"

"Everyone but you. And we missed you! I even heard P. J. Decker asking about you. He was wondering if you were ill. He was the life of the party, Sal. You should have seen him. He did a crazy jazz rendition on the piano with Beaver."

Sally's breath caught in her throat, but Robin continued unawares. "We were all furious when his date dragged him out at midnight. Seems she had other things in mind!"

Sally cringed. How could she have believed P. J. Decker cared for her any differently than he cared for his harem of fans and swooning women. Yet she almost *had* believed it. She almost thought he looked at her with a special light in his eyes. Oh, well, what did it matter anyway? She was a woman with a definite goal in her life. And P. J. Decker was a playboy superstar who basked in the lavish adulation of the throngs. Not a likely duo by any standards.

"Sally? Come back. I lost you again!"

Sally brought her attention back to earth and grinned at Robin as she pushed her through the studio door. "Well, isn't that what producers are for? Come on, let's get cookin'!"

Bill Slater's office was empty when Sally knocked lightly on the door at five minutes before ten. "Well, so much for punctuality." She laughed as she entered and walked over to the long window, waiting for the others to arrive. As she passed the large oak desk, she brushed against a stack of loose papers and they fluttered to the floor. Just as she bent to retrieve them the door opened behind her.

Her back stiffened as a low, husky voice floated down to her. "Funny, but I didn't remember you as being so short."

Pete Decker knelt down beside her, his shoulders rubbing hers, his laughing eyes sweeping over her face as he scooped the papers into a neat pile.

Sally watched him silently. She could feel the warmth of his body. She enjoyed the touch of his shoulder against hers.

"Well, Sally soufflé, how are you? Do you spend a lot of time down here?"

Defenses melted away like butter on hot popcorn. "Oh, Decker . . . hello." She struggled to her feet, seeking the advantage of height, and leaned on the edge of Bill Slater's desk. With relief she heard the approach of voices in the outer office, and in seconds Slater, Beaver, Robin, and Jim Stafford walked through the door.

"Ah, the promptness of my staff astounds me!" boomed Bill Slater, as he settled himself in the soft leather chair behind the desk. "Sit, sit."

The annual weekend meeting at the Lake of the Ozarks resort was planned quickly and the group began to disperse. As Sally tried to slide inconspicuously out the door, P. J. Decker laid a restraining hand on her shoulder and guided her to a quiet corner in the outer office.

"Sally . . ." Those warm cocoa eyes held her again, a glint of amusement flashing in their depths. "I've missed you . . . and I know you've missed me. Why fight it?" He smiled as he spoke, challenging her to deny the electricity that sparked and leaped between them. "Sally . . . I've been waiting patiently for you to make the first move, to give me some sign that you want to pick up where we left off. Say the word."

She looked up and matched his smile. "Decker—you're going to have to cook your *own* goose!"

He laughed, deep and throaty, and caught her in his arms. "That's what I like about you, Sally Denning!" Then, softer, "What do you like about me?"

"A lot, Pete . . . a lot. It's just that you and I, well, we're different . . . our lives, our expectations—so different . . ."

"Yes, and that's what makes it so interesting!" His meaning was clear. Sally tried desperately to hang on to her casual facade and to ignore the dampness collecting in her palms and between her breasts.

"Decker, don't start anything—"

"Don't worry, Sally. I won't start anything I can't finish."

And in a moment he was gone, leaving Sally to cope

with her quickened heartbeat, flushed cheeks, and very frustrated spirit.

Sally walked along the rugged dirt path that lined the water's edge and made her way slowly back to the main lodge. The clear waters of the Lake of the Ozarks lapped lazily against the shore, and in the distance Sally could see two sailboats caught in a gust of unpredictable spring breeze that propelled them flittingly across the surface of the lake.

She loved the Ozark country at this time of year—not yet peopled by tourists and summer folk, blooming and vibrant and quiet. The lake was clean, hushed by winter's freeze and not yet strewn with motorboats and skiers. She remembered the many weekends that the Dennings had spent along the shores of this lake. Remembered Matt teaching them all to water-ski and scale their own fish. Remembered the love in her father's eyes as he watched his clan, proud and strong and every inch the patriarch.

"Hey, Sally! We're starting to load."

Sally pulled herself out of her reveries and looked up the path. She spotted Jim Stafford heading for the lodge parking lot with suitcases in tow. The meeting had been successful, and except for the challenge of avoiding Pete Decker's enigmatic smile, Sally had found herself relaxing and enjoying herself. Now she almost hated to see the weekend end.

"Coming, Jim!" She sprinted up the walkway and joined the assembled group.

"Sally"—Bill Slater pulled her aside—"I have a favor to ask."

"Sure, Mr. Slater. What can I do?"

"Well, I promised P. J. a ride back to his place, but Harry wants me to stay another day and play a couple of rounds of golf with him, which leaves P. J. with a long walk home!"

Sally drew her brows together in a frown and shook her head. "Mr. Slater, I'm afraid that wouldn't be at all convenient. You see,"—her voice gained determination as she continued—"I'm not going straight home either. I'm planning on visiting my father and—"

"I bet P. J. wouldn't mind an afternoon in the country, Sally. Spring Hill, isn't it? Lovely area and besides"—he shrugged apologetically—"I haven't any alternatives up my sleeve."

"What about Beaver and Robin. Surely they can fit a passenger into the jeep," Sally prompted, "even if it means tossing out some of Beaver's junk. You know what a pack rat he is . . ." Her words dangled hopefully.

"Good try, Sally. But Beaver has gone off to hibernate with a six-pack and some cronies from KCKS and Robin left early this morning. I'm afraid you're my, and P. J.'s, only hope."

"Bill, it just won't work. Do *me* a favor and make it a threesome for golf. Could you?"

"Can't do, Sal. Sorry." His eyes lifted from her face and focused on a point just beyond her head. "Well, hi, P. J." He waved. "Just talking about you!"

Sally turned.

Peter was walking toward them. He looked subdued in the unexpected uniform of a suit and tie, but the body was the same, undisguised. The ever-present sensuality and athletic grace. He grinned.

"Hi, Boss. Hello, Sally. Let me tell you I sure felt out of place at these meetings. I'm used to sittin' in my shirt sleeves along one side of some big oak desk, flanked on one side by my agent, and on the other by my attorney, listening to them haggle over my future with some team's business manager who's glaring at me like a trollop eyeing an overpriced diamond."

"Sounds awful to me, Decker!" Sally grimaced, his colorful expression bringing the image clearly to life for her. "But I bet you love every minute of it."

Slater laughed appreciatively, poking one elbow into Pete's good side in a masculine gesture of sympathy. "Heck, I know lots of guys would love to trade places with you."

"Yeah, I know." Pete grinned. "Half of them is in the stands yelling that I'm not worth it and the other half is out on the field trying to prove it!"

"Well, are you worth it?" Sally smiled innocently into his laughing eyes.

"You bet! Worth every penny. Worth every bit of trouble. You know, lady," he teased back, "good things don't come easy!"

One slim brow shot up into the waves of her hair. "Really?" she drawled. "That claim certainly doesn't match your reputation."

Slater slapped his knees and laughed loudly. "That was a 'gotcha' all right, P. J.! Pretty good, Sal!"

They eyed each other through his laughter, measuring, testing, but Slater went right on, unaware of these undercurrents.

"Listen, now that you two are friends again . . ."

They both turned, and he added quickly, "Not that you weren't. It just seemed that things were rather strained there for a while. Anyway," he hurried on, "now I'm sure, Sally, that you won't mind giving P. J. that ride back up to K. C. the way I asked, right?"

"But, Mr. Slater, one thing has nothing to do with the other."

"Listen, Bill, Sally, I don't want to impose."

"No imposition. Right, Sal?" He turned quickly to the other man. "Sally just has a stop to make along the way. You won't mind, will you, P. J.?"

"No, I . . ."

"No, but . . ."

They stopped and waited for the other to continue, the silence hung uncomfortably between them. Sally gave in first.

"If you don't mind getting back late . . ."

"Not at all. If *you* don't mind the company."

"Not at all."

"Good. Then it's settled." Bill winked. "Isn't it nice when we're one big happy family, as Adelle Williams says?" Satisfied with himself, he bit off the end of his cigar and walked away.

Sally also turned to go.

"Sally?" There was a gentleness that tugged at her heart.

"I'm sorry if this is a problem."

She shrugged and smiled with an answering gentleness. "No problem, Pete. Give me about half an hour and I'll meet you in the lobby."

Back in her room she packed quickly and then sat beside her suitcase on the unmade bed. Her fingers played nervously with the satin edging of the blanket. Easy, Sally, she cautioned her troubled psyche. There's no reason why this should unnerve you. You'll give the fellow a lift. He'll wait while you visit Dad. Then you'll take him home and say good night. Easy as pie. This is just four hours we're talking about here, *not* forever. Just keep it cool and uncomplicated. She drew a deep, calming breath, got a good grip on her suitcase, and headed downstairs.

Pete was already there.

"Sorry I kept you waiting," she said with a cool smile intended to demonstrate her ease.

Pete picked up the cue. "Not at all. Plenty of good scenery down here to keep a fellow busy." He smiled lazily at a pair of brunettes who were giving him the eye from across the room. Then he swung his suitcase to his injured side and reached for hers.

"That's all right. I can manage, thank you."

"No doubt about it," he answered, grinning, and followed her out to the car.

Sally handled the little sports car with easy nonchalance. She drove with one hand on the wheel, the other elbow out the window. The sun was hot on her skin and the light dusting of hairs on her arm streamed like peach fuzz in the rushing air. She knew this drive well, each turn, each hill, each narrow one-lane bridge. As a child she had snuggled in the cramped backseat among sleeping bags and picnic baskets on the three-hour journey to and from the lake. To and from weekends spent at the small rented cabin, or occasionally aboard some friend's houseboat. She would play on the cluttered seat behind her two favorite people. Her father was at the wheel, his already graying hair cut in a clean line across his suntanned neck. Matt's sandy, poker-straight hair ended in the same blunt line along his narrow equally tanned neck. The same determined set of the two shoulders. The same fine curve of the two skulls. The same slightly comic thrust of their ears. The repetition was so comforting. Pop and Matt. Matt and Pop. Her two heroes, twin shields against the troubling, incomprehensible world.

The loss of her mother had affected Sally deeply, but there was no woman around to sense her pain. No female to understand and encourage her stifled tears. Above her were Pop and Matt. Their unspoken grief was softened by the dulling simplicity of their similar routines. Work. Home. Sleep. . . . School. Home. Sleep. But Sally, at six, felt the very fabric of her life rip. Gone were the familiar sounds and scents of home, the voice and hands that measured her day. She suffered in silence, afraid that the slightest move would topple the precarious balance of her already tenuous existence. No maidenly aunt arrived. No older sister stepped forward. Pop and Matt. Matt and Pop.

She took her cues from them and held her grief, unexplained and unexplainable, within her.

"That girl needs some other kids her age to play with. That'll help!" Pop announced.

"Yeah. Right." Matt agreed, remembering the gruff comfort of his pals in the junior high locker room.

So Sally left the sudden strangeness of her home and entered the sudden strangeness of preschool. Desperate to please, she was the perfect child, afraid that displeasing would chase away what she had left. Pop and Matt. Matt and Pop. She shadowed them. Adored them. Waited on the front porch until first one, then the other, arrived safely home. Copied them. Mimicked them. She learned quickly what would win their approval—a ball caught and tossed . . . a race won . . . a pair of Matt's jeans worn rolled to the knee, her skinned knees and shins dangling beneath. On field day she brought home blue ribbons. In third grade she joined the soccer team. In fourth she played softball and basketball. In fifth grade she knew the batting averages of every player on the Kansas City Royals baseball team. At the lake she dove the deepest, swam the farthest, caught the most worms, ladybugs, minnows, and lightning bugs. All for Pop and Matt. Matt and Pop. She was the perfect tomboy—one of the guys, one of the family. They had their best times at the lake and on the drives back, when everyone was tired and sunburned and caked with dirt; Pop or Matt would turn from the front seat and flash that same approving smile. Sally would soak it up like sunlight, like life itself. They loved her. They protected her. They would not go away.

But Matt *had* gone. First to college. Then to war, from which he never returned. Then he was forever lost to her sight. And Sally, at fourteen and a half, had held in her grief a second time. She and Pop had suffered alone. Each silent. Unspeaking. Unable to share it. Not knowing how.

And now Pop was going. She knew it. She could feel it,

but she could not face it. Closing the house four years ago seemed to set a clock in motion, a clock that would wind down and stop one day. And with each visit to the old-age home, she could see that day approaching. It was written on his face, in the web of fine wrinkles that lined his skin, in the sudden vacantness of his eyes. Each visit was a joy and a torment. Joy at seeing him again and being together. Torment at seeing him slip away. For each visit she had to gather her energy. She would sift through their shared memories as through a stack of old photos, choosing those that might please him. She would think of jokes and funny sayings to coax a laugh. But what rekindled the old fire in his eyes most surely was drawing him into the world of sports through her retelling of the week's events at the station.

She changed hands on the wheel, brushed the back of her right hand across her wet cheek, and dropped it to the seat at her side. It touched warm flesh.

With a gasp Sally jerked back to the present, to the purr of the engine, the slant of the sun through the windshield, the man beside her. Peter Decker. Long and lean. Quiet. Beneath the thin cotton of his white slacks she could see the outline of his thigh muscles. She cast a quick glance into the rearview mirror. How did she look? Had he been watching her? No, he was staring out the window, his face turned away from her, his hair curled over his neck. His jaw was surprisingly hard, a sharp, etched line. He turned and met her eyes.

"Glad to see you're back with me. I think we were flying on automatic pilot for a while there."

She shrugged and turned her eyes back to the road ahead. "Sorry. I've taken this road so many times before I'm afraid I let my thoughts wander."

"It's okay." He smiled. "Don't apologize. I'm just along for the ride."

She peered at him out of the corner of her eye. Now

94

what had *that* meant? Had there been something in his tone? But his smile was innocent, his eyes warm and honest. She tapped her foot nervously on the gas pedal. "How about you? Do you spend much time at the lake?"

"No. It's hard to find two days free in a row, what with practice, games, PR work. But when I was a kid back in Minnesota . . ." He grinned and shifted on the seat, trying to ease the cramped pain in his injured shoulder. "You know, it seems like yesterday, but when I was a kid, my Grams had a farm near Brainerd. Raised corn and a couple of cows. I had a horse of my own and we used an outhouse! I thought it was heaven."

Sally laughed, caught up in his contagious enthusiasm. "I can see it now! You must have pretended you were some famous pioneer!"

"Frontiersman, woman! I was Daniel Boone and Buffalo Bill Cody rolled up into one. I called the horse Hot Shot and I'd ride him for hours, way out into the woods. Grams would stuff my pockets full of food: jerky and raisins, apples and hunks of chocolate. What a great old gal! I'd bring some pal up with me during the summer—we'd hitch a ride in the back of someone's pickup or borrow my dad's Olds—and we'd spend a week. I'd say, 'Grams, this is Bill or Hank or whatever. Can he call you Grams?' And she'd laugh softly and say, 'Heck, boys, you can call me anything . . . just don't call me late for dinner!' " P. J. chuckled fondly and Sally joined him.

The remembrance had been so real that Sally felt as though the spunky old woman had joined them for a moment there in the car. Wanting to know more, she pushed aside her reticence and asked gently, "Is she still alive?"

"No." He shook his head, his smile dipped down at the corners of his mouth. "No, she died about ten, eleven years ago. I went up one fall weekend and found her there, lying peacefully on that big old wood bed." He looked into

Sally's eyes. "Know something? She never got to see me play pro ball." There was a wistfulness in his eyes that touched a familiar chord in Sally. "I've always been sorry about that," Peter ended softly.

"I bet she would have been damn proud of you!" Sally answered and the strength of her conviction made them both laugh.

"Yeah, you're right." He nodded and leaned back against the door, searching for a comfortable spot to rest his shoulder. "She would have been proud. And sometimes when I hit some really sweet pitch and hear that crack as the ball slides up into the sky, I think, Here, Grams, that one's for you."

"That's nice, Peter," Sally said, fighting to keep her eyes on the road and off his face.

"Well . . . I'm a nice guy."

Again she had to check his intent—and again all she saw was that innocence, that honesty. She laughed and flicked on the radio.

Willie Nelson sang yearningly of love sought and chances lost.

Pete stretched and settled back against the door. "Far to go?"

"Nope. Hey, are you sure that's locked? You shouldn't lean against the door that way."

"Thanks, Mom." He reached over and patted her knee.

"Okay, wise guy, you wait. One good curve and it's good-bye Decker!"

"Hey, that was a compliment. I love my mom." Again that innocent grin, but there was a glint in his eye that betrayed the mischief within.

Sally chose to ignore it. Instead she asked seriously, "Does your mom still live in Minnesota?"

"No. She and my dad moved to Chicago when I first went to play for the Sox. They've got a nice house in Evanston near the lake . . . friends . . . and Dad lectures

96

at Northwestern. So when the Royals picked up my option, they decided to stay there. They figured it was that or spend the rest of their lives following their wayward son from town to town."

"I don't blame them."

"Neither do I." He shook his head emphatically. "They're happy and that's what counts."

"What about you? I mean, do you have any family here in town?"

"No, unless you count the team and all the assorted wives and kids. In some ways we're all a big family." His grin faded and he stared at her, his eyes lingering on the curve of her cheek and lips. When he continued, it was as though he were thinking aloud. "I never thought much about it before. Never missed it . . ."

"Until . . ." Sally prompted hesitantly.

"Until you."

Startled she jerked the wheel to the right and sent the little car sputtering onto the shoulder, kicking loose gravel under its tires. It took her a second to bring it back to the center of her lane. "Decker . . ." she began warningly, but he interrupted.

"Hey, I'm as surprised as you are. And don't take that as a proposal or anything. But you asked and I told you. You've got me feeling things I've never felt before. Thinking about things I hadn't planned on facing for a while yet. I wake up at night remembering how you smell . . . the taste of your kiss . . . the dress you were wearing to the office the day before yesterday, or some such nonsense. And listen to me, telling you about Grams. God, I haven't mentioned her name in years. And now I'm thinking about taking you there. And how it would be to see you standing there in the middle of her pasture, and what you'd think of the old house, and the shelves all lined with teacups. Damn!" He swung his legs back to the floor and set both fists down solid on his knees. "I'm supposed to be thinking about getting this shoulder healed, and keeping my mental state at fever pitch, and here I am burning with some other fever. But"—he grinned, reached over, and twisted one strand of her silky hair around his finger—"I've got to admit . . . I like it."

Sally's heart was beating like a drum against the thin wall of her chest. She fought to quiet it, to keep her attention riveted on the road in front of her, but his words circled her and refused to let go. They soaked into her skin, causing beads of perspiration to gather at her throat and across her forehead. What was he talking about? Didn't he know . . . know that he was P. J. Decker . . . and she was a million miles west of his life . . . on a road traveling in another direction . . . and wouldn't, couldn't, be just a rest stop for him now and then, a brief interlude in the off season. She forced a lightness into her voice and at last found the strength to reply.

"Well, Pete, I think your Grams sounds like a very special woman. I would have loved to have met her. She—"

"Sally . . . Sally . . . Sally . . ." His voice was low.

"What I meant was . . ."

"What you meant was that you'd like to change the subject!" He laughed deep and clear. "Okay, you win. Let's change the subject then. And keep your eyes on the road please, ma'am. Those trees are getting uncomfortably close again."

"Don't you worry about my driving, Mr. Decker. I can handle this car as well as you could."

"No doubt about it!" He slapped his thigh and laughed. "Do you know how many times I end up saying that to you? What is this, major-league competition?"

"Not even minor league, P. J. Don't flatter yourself. What makes you think I'm the slightest bit interested in competing with you?"

"Hey, hold it. What makes you think *I'm* the slightest

bit interested in competing with *you?*" He slid across the seat until his muscular thigh was pressed against hers. His heat radiated through her. She began to melt. "Want to know what I *am* interested in having you do?"

Wild, delicious images filled her brain. His skin against hers. His hands, his mouth. She swallowed, afraid to speak, and pushed against his chest with her shoulder, urging him away.

"What I want you to do"—he breathed against her cheek—"is tell me about you! You've got me mesmerized, hypnotized, and all I've gotten are little glimpses of Sally Denning. Let me see you, Sally. Don't be afraid," he coaxed.

Before she could retort, he laid a hand over hers on the steering wheel. "At least tell me your middle name."

"What?" Again, he had startled her, caught her by surprise. No man had ever been able to throw her so off balance. It made her very nervous.

"My middle name is . . . Madeline." She mumbled it quickly, hoping he wouldn't hear and wouldn't ask again. She should have known better.

"Madeline! That's gorgeous! Perfect! Now tell me, lady, why does that make you blush? Don't you know that suits you?"

"It does not! What do you know about me to make such assumptions? I'm Sally. Sally Denning. I don't know why my parents ever picked such a middle name. Why, it sounds . . . it sounds . . ."

"Positively delightful! Sensuous. Exotic. What else? Mysterious. Alluring. Now listen to me, Sally *Madeline* Denning." His hand tightened over hers, and she could feel the strength of his body. "You're all those things. It's true. I know it and you must know it. I'm no kid, falling for some pretty face and a good pair of legs—though you've got both for sure—there's a depth to you that I don't think even *you've* explored."

"Stop!" She hit the brake and sent the car into a skidding halt. "Stop it! I want you to stop talking this way. Stop looking at me this way. There's no point to it! I don't regret our lovemaking, but it was a fluke. A momentary event. I have my life and you have yours. And they're nothing alike. I had my life just the way I wanted it—well under control—and that's how I intend to have it again. I don't know what you're doing in my car or how you even got here. I should have said no—plain and simple. No! I've had plenty of practice. See? Watch. Read my lips. N-O. But now that you are here I want you to behave. I am going to drive the next forty miles in silence and collect my thoughts and wits. And *you* are going to sit there and watch the scenery, and when we get to my father's rest home, you're going to find a bench under some tree and stay put. I'll only be an hour or so. And then I'll bring you home. Now that's it. Read the script, memorize your part, and you can take a nice bow at the end. Understand?"

His grin was a mixture of sheepishness and devilment. His eyes sparkled and the smooth, shadowed skin of his cheek was creased in a dimple. "Aye, aye, sir!"

A moment's unexplained regret flashed through her as he turned away.

CHAPTER FIVE

The nursing home was set among the rolling farmlands so typical of this part of the Midwest, on the banks of the Little Blue River. The willows were a yellowish-lime green that held the sunlight and dripped it from arched, swaying branches. Dogwood was in bloom, pink and white. Redbud were only flowers, the heavy pink clusters hiding any trace of new leaves. There were no sunflowers yet, just crocus, daffodils, and an abundance of tulips.

Sally drove through Spring Hill; the streets of the tiny town were quiet and deserted on a Sunday afternoon. As she stopped at the one and only stop sign, the sounds of voices mixed with the clatter of silverware, a child's cry, a woman's laugh spilling from one of the houses. She shifted into first and pulled slowly out of town, down the winding county road and under the arched gateway of the Twin Elms Nursing Home.

Before her spread the wide expanse of lawn, dotted with elms and poplars, benches placed invitingly beneath their shade. The lawn sloped up to the front porch of the main building. A new coat of paint sparkled white in the sunlight and green shutters edged the long row of windows.

How many faces watched? How many hands waved in unseen greeting? The porch was a narrow apron circling the house. Cushioned lawn chairs were set in groups of three or four, separated by card tables and a comfortable old porch swing. The main building housed a resident doctor, a staff of nurses, and those residents who needed constant care. Flanking the main building were the cottages where the more mobile residents lived. Each was equipped with linens and kitchenware, comfortable old sofas and easy chairs. Pop lived in 121. He shared the two-bedroom cottage with a wiry old man whom Sally liked a lot. His name was Gustave Lindstrom and he had homesteaded a spread when land cost just a few dollars an acre. The two men argued constantly—over the weather, the economy, tonight's dinner, and, above all, sports. It kept them both on their toes.

Lately Sally had taken to asking Gus for a favor. "Keep an eye on Pop for me this week," she'd say in parting.

"Don't worry, little girl. I'll keep him honest." Gus winked, and Sally felt better.

Today the parking lot behind the main house was already half filled. A sunny Sunday brought the visitors out in droves, and Sally waved to a middle-aged couple she knew. Then she parked, tossed the keys in her purse, and half turned on the seat.

Peter was watching her. His eyes were wide and clear with gentle brown centers that drew her into their depths. "So, your dad lives here?" It was a question, and a statement, said ever so gently.

"Yes. He has for four years now. But it's nice."

"Looks nice." His voice soothed her. "Looks like a fine place to spend the last part of your life."

"Does it?" She scanned her surroundings. "Sometimes it all looks so peaceful, but other times I don't know." Her brow furrowed. "What do you think Grams would have

102

said?" Sally asked the question without knowing she was going to, and regretted it immediately.

Pete narrowed his eyes and looked out into the sun's glare. When he looked back, his voice was thoughtful. "I think she'd say she was glad she died in her own bed, in her own little house, even if she was alone. But, not everyone's that lucky, or that strong, Sally." He hesitated, then forced the words. "Sometimes I think about what it must be like to grow old. To have this body"—he slapped his chest with the flat of one hand—"grow weak and frail, my mind grow vague, to outlive the ones I love and find myself alone." He shook his head. His eyes, still narrowed, searched her face. "I don't like it, Sally. I want something to hold that back. Someone's hand in mine in the dark." His fingers locked around hers. "How about you, Sally Madeline Denning?"

She sat motionless. Not even breathing. Hypnotized. Then she shook off his hand. "I've got to go now. Dad's waiting." She put distance and control back into her voice. "And remember, you're to sit on one of those benches"— she pointed off into the sunlight—"and stay put. I'll just be about an hour."

She slid out of the car, slammed the door, and without another word, headed up the path, her white linen skirt kicking up around her knees.

As she rounded the corner of the porch, she waved to Margaret and Hillary Wentworth, two elderly sisters sitting side by side, on the swing as always. There was Mr. Llewlyn, Bert Fells, and Jay Myers, hard at a three-handed game of rummy. Piers Brandt hobbled toward her with his wooden cane. "Good morning, missy," he greeted her in his rich Dutch accent. "I've not seen your dad today, but you tell him for me I want a rematch at horseshoes."

"Will do, Mr. Brandt. See you later."

She liked these people and enjoyed her time here. She had been known to pick up the fourth hand of cards, toss a horseshoe herself, learn a few crochet stitches from Wanda Olfant. She could sit and listen for hours to the stories they had to tell. Someday she'd write them down and catch these lives on paper.

Her heels tapped a light staccato rhythm across the path to 121. The old wooden knocker echoed so that even failing ears could heed its call. And sure enough, from the other side of the door came a slow, heavy step.

"Gustave! Hello, it's me, Sally." The door swung wide and Sally was engulfed in a tender hug.

"Ah, Sally. So good to see you! We missed you last week. But I told Lou you'd be here for sure today. Come on in. Hey, Lou. Guess who's here!"

Sally followed the old man into the kitchen. Lou Denning sat in a straight-back chair facing the window. He was wrapped in a bathrobe and his gray hair stood in sleep-tousled tufts around his head. But the years fell away as he turned and saw Sally in the doorway.

"Ah . . . sweetie" He started to rise but Sally was faster. She hurried to his side, wrapped her arms around his shoulders, and placed a kiss on his cheek.

"Hello, Pop. Oh, I've missed you. I'm so sorry about last weekend. Did Gertrude give you the message?"

"Gertrude? That old biddy couldn't give you her right name! What message?"

Sally glanced at Gustave who nodded over Lou's head.

"Never mind, Pop. I'm just glad to be here now. How've you been?"

"Fine and dandy, except for the food, Sal. You know, I think they're trying to do us in. Ask Gus. Where did he get to, anyway?"

"I'm right here, Lou."

"What are you doing lurking in the corner? Get yourself a chair and sit down! I don't know, Sal"—he lowered his voice in a stage whisper that could have been heard outside—"Gus has been acting kind of funny lately, don't you think?"

"Now, Pop." Sally hushed him, but Gus winked away her discomfort and straddled a third chair.

"You old coot! Afraid to say things to my face?"

"Me? Afraid of you? Why, I could punch out your lights with one hand tied behind my back. Just step outside. Come on!"

"Time!" Sally flashed the umpire's familiar signal. "Pops, why don't you get dressed and we'll go out for a walk?"

"Walk? This early? Bet the dew's not even dry. You're trying to get me pneumonia or something."

"It's the middle of the afternoon, Dad. The sun is out and it's lovely. Now go on, I'll wait here."

"Of course you'll wait there. What did you think you were going to do. Come get me dressed like some baby? I don't know . . ." This time his baleful eye was turned on Sally and his whisper directed at Gus. "Sometimes she sure acts funny, don't you think?"

Sally and Gus shared an affectionate chuckle as Lou headed for the bedroom. Then Sally asked softly, "Has everything been all right, Gustave?"

"Right as rain, Sally. He's doing fine, there's no need to worry."

Sally forced a smile of thanks, then quickly changed the subject. "How about your supplies. Can I get you two anything from town?" She rummaged through the closets, jotting items on a scrap of paper: Saltines . . . cereal . . . soup. Anything else? Would you like some more tobacco, Gustave?"

"That'd be nice, Sally. And how about some fruit?"

"Okay, I'll bring you something ripe and juicy."

"Nope. At my age I better settle for peaches!"

Sally laughed. "You're the greatest!"

"Ain't that what I've been telling you for two years, missy?"

When Lou returned, Sally linked her arm through his and headed outdoors.

"Hmmm, that sun sure does feel good. What time did you say it was?"

"Mid-afternoon, Pop. It is nice, isn't it?"

They circled the grounds. Sally matched her step to her father's. They stopped often, to rest on a bench, greet a friend, talk. As they passed the porch, a chorus of hellos surrounded them.

Lou ducked his head and trudged on.

"Pop! That wasn't nice. Why didn't you say hello?"

"Say hello?" The old man scowled at her. "Did you see that Wanda Olfant? She's got her sights set on me. One nice word and she's off and running. Well, she can run all she wants, but she won't catch me." He laughed gleefully, turning to wave a mocking hand at the veranda. "Bye-bye, Wanda!"

"Pop!"

"Don't 'Pop' me. I'm telling you, that woman is something else. That reminds me. I knew there was somethin' I needed to talk to you about. Come sit down here, Sal— this is important."

Sally followed him to a bench in the shade of a forsythia bush.

"Listen, missy. That Wanda Olfant, she came bustlin' over yesterday. No? The day before. No . . . maybe . . . oh, what the heck! I don't remember exactly *when* it was, but she was bristlin' with news like some porcupine with its quills all adither. Said she saw you on the TV."

Sally paled, and her hands clutched nervously at her purse strap. "Oh, really? Did she like me?" she asked, feigning innocence.

"Like you? She thought you were the cat's meow! Came over to tell me. Let's see, how'd she put it, the old sow?

106

Yeah, I remember . . ." His voice rose to a shrill falsetto as he imitated the elderly spinster. " 'Oh, Lou, you have such a darling daughter . . .' Ugh!" He grimaced, shaking all over like a dog shedding water. "Darling daughter? What does she think, I raised some flouncy little thing with her hair all in curls . . . 'darling daughter' . . . she made you sound like Shirley Temple! And you know what else? She said you were giving a cooking lesson!"

Sally flinched, but Lou never noticed. He went right on. "She said you were stuffin' some bird or something. Well, I told her, 'Get out of here you old bird, before I stuff you!' Cooking lesson! *My* daughter is on the sports show! Every night! Channel six! Right? Ha, ha! Cooking show! I got a good laugh out of that." His laugh was fierce and Sally felt it pummeling her eardrums and temples.

"Listen, Dad." She waited until she had his attention, then wiped her damp palms on the front of her skirt.

"I'm listening, missy. What are you looking so serious about?"

"Well"—she forced a smile—"it's not *that* serious. It's just that I have something to explain. Things have been so busy, and then I didn't see you last week, and—"

"Get to it, girl. No need to keep running bases when the ball has been caught!"

"Well . . ." Sally moistened her lips with the tip of her tongue. Her throat was painfully dry. "Lots of things have been happening up at the station. And, temporarily . . ." She wished she could underline the word, print it in big fat letters so he'd be sure to understand it, "Temporarily I am doing the cooking show. Something came up and Mr. Williams had to juggle the staff so . . ."

"So! So what! You're on the sports show!" His voice carried across the lawn and Sally laid a restraining hand on his knee, but Lou ignored it and ranted on, "Don't you let anyone take away your job. A man's job is his most important possession. You fight for that, Sal. I'm telling you! Who does that Williams think he is? Why, I'd like to just go up there and punch his lights out for him! And who is this clown who took your place? If I got my hands on him . . ."

Sally was filled with the same irrational desire. If Decker had been there she could have wrapped her hands around his throat and strangled him! Look at the chaos he had caused. Oh, damn! Damn it all! It took a great effort to push aside her own dismay and calm her father. "Dad, please listen, it's only temporary."

"Sal, you've got to fight for your rights. Oh, if only I was some help instead of some dried-up old coot stuck in this place. Listen"—his eyes glittered wildly—"I've got an idea! How about if I come live with you. I'll do the cooking and take care of the place, and then you can go get your job back and . . ."

Again Sally strove to restrain him. "Hush, Dad, please, it's all right. Please sit down and lower your voice."

"I don't want to sit down! What do you think I am anyway? I'm your father, little girl. I'll give the orders here, if you please!"

"Yes, Dad, of course. Just please . . ."

"No!" Lou broke from her grasp and with head lowered he shuffled back toward the path.

Sally raced to his side, unaware of the tears that stained her cheeks. "Pop, please sit down and let's talk."

"No! Treat me like a baby, that's what you do! Think I'm no use at all." He turned abruptly and wrapped his gnarled arms around Sally's shoulders, hugging her close, but not before she saw the tears filling his eyes. "Sal, you're my little girl. You'll always be my little girl. And I only want to help make you happy, but I feel so helpless. There's just nothin' I can do."

"Oh, Pop." Sally let her cheek rest against his shoulder. "Mr. Denning?"

Sally gasped and Lou whirled toward the voice, almost

108

losing his balance on the uneven slope of the lawn. But Peter stepped off the path and caught his arm.

"What? Who?" Lou glared up into the young man's face and Sally saw his sadness dissolve into recognition. "Hey! You're P. J. Decker! I'd know you anywhere." His hand clutched eagerly at Pete's arm.

"Yes, sir," Pete said softly.

Lou stared him in the face for a full minute, then broke into a grin. "Hey, Sal"—he motioned to her, his other hand still holding tight to Pete as if afraid he might disappear—"Sal, look who I found! This is P. J. Decker!"

"I know, Pop." Sally stepped unwillingly to his side.

"Sure you know. You're on the sports show! Every night! Channel six. Hey, P. J., this is my girl, Sally."

"Yes, sir. I know. She's lovely."

Sally blushed furiously but Lou only beamed proudly. Then in a conspiratorial whisper he added as an afterthought, "Hey, P. J. you should see her pitch! Damn good right arm."

Pete threw back his head and laughed, and Lou, pleased with his effect, joined him. Sally backed away, but Lou plucked possessively at her sleeve.

"Here, missy, listen. Maybe P. J. Decker can help you get your job back. What do you say, P. J.?"

"Mr. Denning, you have my word. I'll see that Sally gets her job back just as soon as possible."

"There!" Lou chortled, immeasurably pleased with himself. "See, Sal, P. J. Decker will help you! Nothing like a good man to set things right!"

Her blood boiling, her hands clenched into fists at her side, Sally followed the two men back up the path. Through her veil of anger, she saw Peter's fair head bent attentively to her father's gray one. The ball player held lightly to Lou's elbow, guiding and supporting him without hovering. Lou tried to hurry along, calling to those on the porch from yards away, "Folks! Look who's here! P.

J. Decker! Hey, Bert, Jay. Look, it's P. J. Decker. Wanda, come here. Let me introduce this young fellow."

Sally stood in the shadow cast by the porch railing. Dark clouds began filling the sky, chasing away the sunlight. In front of her the older people mobbed Pete, reaching out to touch him, lifting their voices in greeting. At their center stood Lou, grinning ear to ear. His shoulders were straight, his chest puffed with pride. Sally wanted to be angry, bitter that Pete Decker had pushed his way into another dimension of her life, forced his way into her father's affections. She wanted to cry out to her father that P. J. Decker was a fake, that it was *his* fault she had lost the job Lou Denning was so proud of! But she stood in silence, unable to muster the anger, the hurt. Lou Denning was happy, excited, and having the time of his life. What good would it do to rob him of that moment?

The first drops of rain began to fall an hour later. The old folks and their visitors scattered quickly, scurrying back to the cottages and into the dim twilight of the main building's foyer. Lou rubbed a hand over his thin hair and laughed.

"Look at 'em all run. Like a flock of chickens when a hawk sails by." He smiled companionably at Pete as together they watched the retreating figures. "Must be afraid they'll melt." He chuckled.

Sally grinned, in spite of herself. Only she, Pop, and Pete were left. "Perhaps we'd better join them, Pop."

Lou smiled and climbed slowly to a porch chair just out of the rain's reach. "Sal, I think I've had enough excitement for one day." He peered into the slanting curtain of rain. "Ain't going to stop, Sal. I can tell." He winked at Pete. "When I was a young man out farming my land, I could tell when a storm was blowing up. Knew it before the weathermen. Once I predicted a twister a good half hour before the county sirens started blowing."

The door behind them creaked open and Wanda stuck her head out. "Radio says there's a bad storm on its way. One inch hail and high winds," she recited ominously, then disappeared back inside.

"See, what did I tell you. Right on cue. You better head home, missy." Suddenly confused, he looked over at Pete. "Hey, P. J., I forgot to ask, who are you visiting? I mean, no one said you were coming and you being a celebrity and all . . ."

"I'm with Sally, Mr. Denning. She's giving me a lift home."

"No fooling! Well"—he straightened in his chair and nodded sagely—"I should have known, what with Sally being on the sports show every night, channel six and all, she's sure to know some big-shot ball player." He reached over and patted Sally's knee. "That was great, you keepin' it a surprise for me that way."

Sally smiled wearily and covered his hand with hers. "Glad you had a good afternoon, Pop."

"Good? It was great! Best I've had in years!" He rose stiff-legged from the chair. "Time to get home. Now, you two go on. Drive carefully."

Sally hugged him tightly. She could feel the brittle framework of his bones. Again her eyes misted. "You take care. I love you, Pop," she whispered against his shoulder.

"You, too, little girl. Good-bye, P. J., and I'm going to hold you to your promise now. You help Sally get her job back, you hear?"

"Will do, sir, I promise. And it was an honor meeting you."

"Thank you, son."

Sally raced through the rain to her car and Pete slid in beside her. They were both drenched to the skin, their hair plastered to their foreheads and cheeks. Pete took one look at her and began to laugh. "There was a little girl, who had

111

a little curl . . ." he teased, fingering the outline of the damp curl stuck to the center of her forehead. His laugh was infectious.

Sally heard herself answering, "And when she was good . . ."

But before she could finish, Peter leaned over, pressing his chest to her wet blouse. His mouth covered hers with steamy, tempting kisses. ". . . she was marvelous," he murmured against her parted lips.

Sally's nipples hardened under the wet silk of her blouse. She returned his kiss, then leaned back, mischief shining in her eyes. ". . . and when she was bad . . . she was better!"

Pete's eyes flew wide in surprise. Sally clapped a hand over her mouth. "I didn't mean to say that, Decker! Don't you get any ideas now."

"Too late, Sally soufflé. I've already got 'em!"

They laughed, their bodies tangled together in the front seat of the tiny car. The windows were all steamed, whether from the rain or their warm breath, she couldn't be sure. Finally Sally slid back against the door, opening a space between them. "Decker, what are you? A magician? Or a snake charmer? I had every intention of being angry with you. Telling my father *you'd* help me get my job back!"

Pete's low laugh whipped up her desire. "I'm both, my sweet." He shot a sexy look in her direction. "Now let's head home while I've still got you under my spell."

They drove through the lowering darkness of storm and twilight. After a long period of comfortable silence, Sally's gaze moved to the man on the seat beside her. Pete was leaning his head back against the door. His right hand cradled his left, just above the elbow. There was a tightness about his mouth that spoke of pain. A sudden fear filled Sally.

"Are you all right, Peter?"

His brown eyes opened and swept her face. "Sure. And I'll be even better once we're home. Afraid I overdid things this weekend, and now the rain has this damn shoulder aching."

"Does it hurt a lot?"

"Some. But I'm tough." He grinned. "Don't worry. I'll be fine, Sally." He let his lids droop, but his husky voice drifted across to her. "See, Sally, I knew it! Deep down in your heart, although you try damn hard to hide it, you really *do* like me."

Sally arched one brow. "Perhaps I'd better plead the Fifth, on grounds it might incriminate me!"

"Well, I like you, Ms. Denning. And I was just thinking, if we were to get married, you wouldn't have to change the initials on your towels."

"Marry you? *Marry* you!" Sally sputtered, both hands flying off the wheel.

"Okay, okay! No need to get excited. It was just a thought." He watched her, enjoying the flush that rose to her face. He found himself enjoying a lot of things about this enigmatic young woman who had invaded his life. He grinned across at her in the darkness.

The storm pounded at the little car. Occasionally a white arc of lightning lit the sky, throwing into stark relief a house, a telephone pole, the empty road ahead. Sally was forced to keep her mind on the road now. She had decided it was the only safe place anyway, but her body ignored that decision. She was totally aware of his presence.

At last she saw the turnoff for the county road. She pulled to a stop in front of Peter's house. "Okay, Mr. Decker. End of the line for you."

Pete reached over and in one swift movement turned the ignition off and pocketed the key. "And a coffee break for you." As she began to object, he continued, "Nope, Sally. I saw those beautiful lids dropping ten miles back. I can't let you go on in this weather, at least not without a cup of Decker's coffee."

"Well,"—Sally softened—"I could use a pick-me-up, maybe even a stale piece of toast. Thanks, Pete."

They walked through the house, trailing puddles of water from entryway to kitchen. Pete stopped along the way to grab two fluffy terry towels, one of which he wrapped gently around Sally's head and shoulders. "Want a robe?" he offered.

"No, no!" Sally answered quickly. "I won't be staying that long, sir. Cup of coffee, remember?"

"Shucks!" He grinned. "Why don't you curl up on the screened porch and keep a watch on the weather."

In a short time he had joined her, carrying a tray heaped with hunks of cheese, fruit, an array of crackers, two steaming mugs of coffee, and a bottle of brandy. He poured a generous splash of the liqueur into his own coffee, then held the bottle poised over hers. "What do you say, Sally?"

She gave an uncertain shrug of her wet shoulders.

"I'll take that as a yes, and remember, this house has lots of places to rest a weary head."

Sally sipped at her coffee, eyeing him over the rim of her cup. The wetness had added to his sensuality. His clothes were molded to his body. She saw through them. Saw him naked. Aroused. Desiring her. Saw him as he had been curled next to her that night, on the Navaho rug before the fire. The hot coffee burned her lips but she needed an excuse to swallow. Was it her tiredness that made her so vulnerable? The confusion of the day that made her so susceptible? She knew better.

Peter pared off a slice of cheese and handed it to her on a cracker. Their fingers touched and she was weak. He refilled her cup, adding more brandy, and she didn't stop him. The warmth filled her, weighing heavily upon her limbs. If her lids had drooped before, they were leaden now. She pushed away from the table and stood. "Come on, Decker. I need to go for a walk."

He looked at her quizzically. "A walk? It's still raining, Sally."

Sally laughed and plucked teasingly at her blouse. The soaked material pulled reluctantly away from her breasts, then billowed back and stuck once again to her flesh. "Oh? Are you afraid I'll get wet?"

Pete rose, that wolfish smile spreading across his face. "You do have a point there. Well, I'm with you, kid. Lead on."

"No, you first. You seem to be pointing the way."

They dissolved in laughter, falling into each other's arms as they tumbled out the door.

When he could speak again, Pete grinned down at her. "You are a little devil. I think I need a chaperon!"

"Oh? I thought you said you were tough, Decker."

He gathered her to him, wrapped an arm about her, and gathered her to his side. "Maybe not as tough as I thought," he whispered, and kissed her hair.

Rain streamed down their bodies. It was warm and gentle now, a shimmering veil hanging over the backyard and the lake beyond. Pete led her down an old stone path toward the lake's edge. "This is nice." He smiled, then pulled her into a clearing surrounded by the heavy, dripping shapes of old trees. A wide rope hammock was suspended between two gnarled oak trees, the uppermost branches forming a leafy roof.

Peter settled carefully onto the hammock's center and held out his arms. "Come to me, Sally."

Sally perched carefully on the hammock's edge and leaned down into his arms. The hammock tipped sideways under her weight. "I don't think I trust this thing." She laughed nervously.

"Trust me!" Peter leaned forward and wrapped his

arms around her, drawing her down on top of him. Again the hammock swung wildly.

"Peter! Careful."

"Shhh, darlin'. I intend to be very careful—and very slow—and it will be very good." He cupped his hands around her face and kissed her, gently at first, his lips moving softly over hers, pressing and lifting with great tenderness.

Sally returned his kiss as her tongue traced the outline of his lips, probed the sweet corners of his mouth. Then she drew away but he followed, his mouth clinging to hers, forbidding her to go. She knew she should get up. She should get in her car. She should drive back to Lawrence and the safety of her own small apartment. But the rain had washed away the "shoulds" as surely as the brandy had melted her defenses and fired her desire. She cradled the curve of his head in her palms, entwined her fingers in his hair. "Oh, Decker. What are you doing to me?"

"Wait and see. This is just the first inning, my sweet soufflé." His arms tightened their hold, his kiss deepened. He slid his hands across her drenched back and down her arms, then curved around her ribs and met at the top button of her blouse. He sank back into the hammock, leaving her leaning above him. His eyes smiled into hers. His lips were parted. His chest rose and fell in deep, uneven breaths. Slowly he undid the first button, then the next, and each in the row until the silk parted and her wet cream-colored skin was bare. Tugging gently at the silk, he peeled the blouse down around her shoulders, free of one arm, then the other, and tossed it to the end of the hammock. His fingers returned to unfasten her bra. He moaned softly as the flimsy web released her soft, full breasts to the rain's touch.

Sally had stayed so still the hammock had not stirred. She was mesmerized by his touch. Now his broad hands on her naked back drew her back toward him and at the same time he curved up toward her. His mouth found the tender hollow of her throat. He kissed her there, then trailed his mouth down over the wet, taut skin of her shoulders, down around the swelling sides of her breasts. She felt the delicious hot wetness of his mouth moving across the undersides of her breasts. He nuzzled into the cleavage between. His tongue rasped across first one nipple, then the other.

Sally bit her lips in delight, shivering as his tongue circled and probed. In its path the rose-colored flesh puckered and crinkled. Her nipples hardened and ached.

Pete cupped his hands around the fullness of her flesh and drew his face back and forth across the sensitized peaks. She felt the brush of his hair, the prickly roughness of his unshaven cheek, that rasping tongue. "Oh, lady," he said softly, shakily. "You are lovely. I love the feel of you . . . and the taste of you . . . and the way you respond when I touch you."

"So glad you approve," she answered in a throaty whisper. "Because I really can't help it, Peter," she confessed in a hushed tone. "You just look at me sometimes and I . . ."

"Really?" He tipped his head back and offered a slow, sexy smile. "I just look at you . . . and what happens, sweet Sally?" he prompted.

"And . . ." she began, but then stopped herself. She gazed down at him with a soft smile, her hand coming up to stroke his damp cheek. "You really are an impossible man, Decker."

"Maybe . . ." His voice trailed off on a deep sigh as his hands pulled her up, across his body. "Maybe I just need a woman who knows how to handle me." His tongue darted out to lick the straining, swollen tips of her breasts. "Handle me, sweet Sally," he whispered huskily. "You don't know what you do to me . . ." Round and round his warm lips circled, nipping, sucking, until Sally writhed in

117

ecstasy, aware of nothing but his touch and the fact that her body was on fire.

With a moan she tumbled back and the hammock lurched crazily into space. Peter shifted quickly, caught hold of both sides, and steadied them.

A husky laugh rumbled in his throat. "Perhaps I'd better steer." He drew her to the center of the hammock, stripped off his shirt, and pressed her back, his warm, rough chest against her yielding breasts as he looked down into her eyes. "What we've got here, love, is a very delicate balance."

"But I thought we were floating," she teased, circling his neck with her arms. "You're the magician. I'll leave it all in your hands."

"Oh, Sally, I would do magic for you. I will." He kissed her hard then slid down over her like the rain, touching, tasting, licking the raindrops from the light curve of her belly.

She felt his hands slide beneath the waistband of her skirt. And again the world fell away. Trees and branches. Rain and wind. And the hammock tilting, swinging. She moved to the rhythm of his urging, the rhythm of her own desire. When he leaned away to remove the last remnants of her clothing and his, she stroked his back and arms, feeling the muscles tighten beneath her fingers as he hurried.

Then they were pressed length to length, the stroking of his fingers replaced by the urgent demand of his thighs and hips, the spurring hardness of his passion. Hungrily his mouth covered hers in a kiss fierce and demanding. The world narrowed, focused in the pulsating center of her being. She tilted her head back and wrapped her legs around his. She ached with desire and urgent need.

"Peter," she whispered. "Peter . . . I want you—love me now . . ."

He tore his mouth from hers and looked down at her

with pain and love and desire mixed in his eyes. "And I want you, Sally."

Sliding his hands beneath her hips, he raised her gently, slowly toward him. She held her breath in rapt anticipation. Then she felt the sweet, burning fullness of him sliding within her. And it *was* magic.

The rain was a coating of warm honey on their bodies. The hammock was an angel's wing carrying them to heaven. Peter found and claimed the sweet, hidden corridors of her being until he knew her body's intricate ways and passages. Lovingly, with murmurs and urgent hands, she guided him, bringing him closer and closer, stroking his face, his hips, his shoulders, memorizing him, absorbing him, until he filled her every crevice. And there was the last door . . . the last barrier . . . and he burst within. And she welcomed him.

The hammock slowed and swayed in gentle undulation. Sally curled against him, snuggling close to the heat of his body.

He kissed her hair and wrapped his arms around her, curving his body like a shield against the night breeze.

They lay like that for a while. Sally felt the world drift back. Rough dark trunks. Wet grass. The loose webbing of the rope against her skin. And more. The house beyond. The lake. The day now drawn to a close. She was aware of a new stillness, a sureness within her that nothing could touch. Like a calm lake this new feeling lay, unruffled by wind or tide or time. She turned and wrapped her arms around his back, leaning her cheek against his chest. She fitted snug. Just right. As if she were made to be there. As if he were made to hold her.

Later he whispered into her hair, "Sally, my sweet Sally, let's go inside."

She stirred, uncurled, but continued to lie against him. "I'm happy here."

"Let's go be happy inside, love. I'm cold."

"Funny. I'm warm." She smiled into the darkness.

"Nothing funny about it. You've got me wrapped around you like a blanket."

"All right, then. I'll just wear you inside." She slipped an arm about his waist and together they half climbed, half slipped from the hammock's embrace.

"God, that was a first." Pete laughed softly as they headed back up the path.

Sally stopped and peered into his face. "Really? At first I was afraid it was a favorite old haunt."

He shook his head slowly, smiling. "Nope. You're the only one worth the risk."

Sally grinned and started to walk on, but he held her still.

"And what about me, Sally? Am *I* worth the risk?"

Rising on tiptoe, she planted a light kiss on his chin. "I am beginning to think so."

Inside he found her a top from a pair of his pajamas, and wore the bottom part himself. He poured them each a stiff brandy, then flopped across the wide four-poster bed in his bedroom. "Come here," he said, patting the old patchwork quilt beside him.

Sally paused and slid her hands over the intricate carvings on the maple. "What a beautiful old bed, Peter. Was it Grams's?"

"Nope. Grandfather Decker's. Now come on in here, girl."

"I don't know. I feel a little funny, getting into your grandfather's bed."

"Don't. He was something of a rake himself."

CHAPTER SIX

The euphoria of the baseball crowd was contagious, and no person in the dense throng that made its way down the aisles in the huge stadium escaped its spell. The pungent odor of beer, mixed with the spiciness of hotdogs and onions welcomed the fans; the cries of the vendors enveloped them as they made their way down to their seats.

Sally shivered and pulled her electric-blue sweater about her. She knew it wasn't the breeze that caused the sensation, it was the baseball magic. It caught her and wrapped her tightly, raising her to its frenzied level of anticipation.

It *was* in her blood, she thought, settling down beside Beaver and Robin in their front-row seats. It was her past and her present. But what was the future to bring? A tinge of confused emotion swept through her. The sportscaster's job was never very far from her thoughts. Everyone was quick to remind her she'd have it back soon, but in the hectic, dog-eat-dog world of television, nothing was ever certain. You got what you could, and held on tightly. She hadn't even had the chance to get a good, solid grip on the job. But was she willing to let go of what she *now* held in her hands, and in her heart?

"Where do you suppose P. J. is?" Robin's voice edged her way into Sally's consciousness.

P. J. The name still caused a quickened heartbeat, even though Sally's involvement with Pete Decker had become an accepted state of affairs at the office. During the weeks that followed that wondrous night in the hammock, Sally had gradually given vent to her feelings and emotions, letting down some of the old barriers and hoping the future would somehow take care of itself. She felt a budding within herself that slowly permeated her whole body, revealing a new side to Sally Denning that she found herself liking more and more. And she knew with unspoken certainty that Pete Decker's intrusion into her life was responsible for the way she felt.

At first, Pete's attentions had frustrated Sally, but his charm and humor and the feelings that flooded Sally when she saw him washed away the discomfort. Admittedly there were a few times when Sally would gladly have done without quite so much solicitude. Like the day Pete arrived at the office with a "small momento," as he called it. A half smile curved her lips as the scene flashed before her eyes.

She and Pete had enjoyed a wonderful early summer picnic the night before and Sally was still basking in its afterglow when Pete approached her that day at the office. He very ceremoniously placed an enormous, gift wrapped box marked "For Emergency Use Only" on her desk. Under the bemused gaze of the entire staff, she had torn away the cardboard, exposing a six-foot-wide Pawley's Island hammock. It took Sally quite a bit of explaining and fancy footwork to get it back into the box and away. Decker only stood on the sidelines, a slow seductive smile on his face.

Any attempts to thwart his overt attentions were merely

fuel for the fire. And the fire continued to grow and grow, filling Sally with a wondrous warmth. And in those moments when she was alone and the old guarded confusion and restraint crept into her thoughts, she managed to tuck it carefully back under its cover, promising herself she would deal with it another time, another day.

Sally couldn't even remember now when Pete's attentions ceased to embarrass her and instead began filling her with quiet delight. Perhaps it was the day he had planted two dozen roses in the studio microwave, along with *very* sensual directions on how to make rose hip tea. To the delight of her TV audience, Sally had unwittingly unveiled the surprise in the middle of her telecast.

Or it could have dissolved on their long walks along the shaded banks of Lake Winnepeg . . . or during Pete's frequent visits to *The Back Burner* set that had been quietly woven into the pattern of Sally's life as subtly as the blossoms on the branches outside her window. Or maybe it had become smothered in the embers of desire as Sally found herself yearning more and more for the delight of Pete's touch and rejoicing in the fierce joy of his lips upon her own.

"Sally?" Robin tapped Sally's arm lightly and jerked her back to the ball park. "Welcome back, dear. Wherever you were you certainly seemed to be enjoying yourself!"

Sally chuckled. "Sorry, Robin. You know me—dizzy dreamer! But in answer to your question—Pete said he had to see someone for a few minutes but would join us here shortly."

Satisfied, Robin went back to reading her program while Sally settled back into the seat. Her deep blue eyes swept the stands, resting on the expanse of brilliant green turf spread out before her. The ground crew was busy with brooms, touching up the bases and the pitcher's mound. Several players from either team tossed balls back and forth, while others stretched their impressive muscles, bending, pulling, straightening. Sally watched them with a practiced eye. She enjoyed the movements as if they were part of some grand ballet being danced before her.

And yet the drama was always new, always filled with the thrill of expectation. Sally settled back with the ease and appreciation of a veteran.

The Royals' dugout was a stone's throw from Sally's seat, and out of the corner of her eye she could see the players moving in and out while the bat boys lined up the tools of the trade, proudly showing off in front of the crowd. She recognized the catcher, Joey Rao, his thick black hair curling out from beneath his helmet as he climbed out of the dugout. A broad-shouldered, plaid-shirted man followed him, his clothes sharply contrasting with the blue and white of the Royals' uniform. He stood next to Rao, then turned slightly. A roar went up from the portion of the noisy crowd nearby and was soon taken up and echoed around the stadium. "P. J.! P. J. We want P. J.! Welcome back!"

Sally's heart jerked and she strained to see the two men standing on the far side of the dugout. Peter stood next to his friend, a smile playing across his lips as he faced his fans and waved. But Sally watched his eyes. She caught the look that shone from their depths. He was hurting. Peter Decker didn't belong in a plaid shirt—with a bum shoulder—as baseball moved into the height of the season. He belonged behind third base, his eye on the ball, his back arched, his feet poised for action. Sally cringed. This was his life. And it had been cruelly jerked away from him by the same hand of fate that had been so unyielding with her. She could feel his anguish as she searched the depths of his eyes and the look that spread across his handsome face. Suddenly Sally felt that she needed to touch him, to soothe him, to tell him it would be all right. She *would* help him through it, until he was once again dressed in the Royals' blue and white uniform.

His eyes met hers as he scanned the crowd and he paused, trying to read her expression. He whispered something to Rao, waved once more to the fans, then walked over to the fence in front of Sally and, using his good arm, hoisted his long frame over the barricade. A uniformed security guard sped over, then stopped in his tracks as he recognized the transgressor. "P. J., howdy! How's that shoulder comin'? Sure is good to see you back here!" P. J. smiled an answer to the white-haired guard, then moved swiftly to Sally's side.

She blushed as he planted a kiss lightly on her forehead under the curious scrutiny of dozens of people in the stands, then slid down to the hard metal seat at her side.

"Hi, Pete." She smiled. "Are you all right? I—I was worried about you for a moment." She hesitated, unsure of what or how much to say here. She felt suddenly awkward with this man beside her, her emotions fluctuating as quickly as Kansas weather. He was a star, a baseball hero, back on his own turf.

But Peter brushed away her fears and insecurities. "I'm fine, honey. Don't you worry." He wrapped an arm lightly over her shoulders, found a comfortable position for his injured shoulder, and struck up a friendly discussion with Beaver about the Yankees' rookie pitcher who was making his first start against the Royals that night.

Sally relaxed, happy in the pleasure of the moment and determined to let deeper feelings rest for now.

Soon all four of the WQEK staff were caught up in the excitement of the game. When the Royals played the Yankees, it was always a match full of heightened tension and excitement. Kansas City fans were determined not to let the Big Apple fans outdo them and proudly defended their honor, yelling, screaming, and cheering their team on to victory over the dreaded Eastern foes.

Peter leaned over. "Watch this guy, Sally. Lennie Dawe. He's our newest rookie. Plays outfield and can

125

really swing a bat. This is his first time at the plate." Pete's voice was filled with excitement and pride and a kind of vicarious thrill.

Sally watched the tall, well-muscled youth approach the plate. His blond hair flopped down on his forehead and he brushed it away with the back of his hand. She caught her breath. For a moment she was Sally Denning, twelve and a half years old, sitting in the Lawrence stadium as Matt Denning, all-star college baseball player, came up to bat. Then she was back with the rookie, watching as he bent at the waist, poised his bat for the swing. His stance, his body, all were an echo of Matt's. With the brazenness of youth, the young player grinned at the pitcher, took a deep breath, and swung hard as the fast ball flew across the plate. Contact echoed in the stands. The ball tore down the left-field line. The player slid into second base. Safe. The scoreboard lit up and the crowd went crazy as they read the flashing letters. LENNIE DAWE AVG. 1,000!!! Sally joined the crowd in wild cheers, brushing away the tears before anyone would notice.

"Didn't I tell you, Sally? He's terrific. What a thrill for that young kid."

"Yes," Sally whispered. "What a thrill."

Peter frowned at her for a moment, then let his attention be drawn back to the field. The game was a pitchers' duel. Except for the Royals' one run following the rookie's double, the scoreboard was idle. And when the final out was made, a cheering, boisterous crowd poured out of the ball park with a 1–0 home victory under their belts.

Beaver stood and stretched as the two women gathered up their sweaters and purses. "Well, where to now, P. J.?"

"Now, my friends, we are about to crash the annual 'Damn Yankees' party."

"What?" Robin's eyes opened wide.

"Yep. Our 'Damn Yankees' bash. Each year, after the first battle between the two teams, a loyal fan throws this

126

party for all of us, Yankees and Howard Cosell excluded! It's always a lot of fun, and with a victory under our belts, you can bet the champagne will flow tonight."

Following P. J.'s instructions, Beaver expertly maneuvered his jeep along the luscious winding streets of Mission Hills. The affluent Kansas City suburb boasted wooded, rolling hills, curving lanes, and fountains and statues to rival those of Rome. Behind the clusters of carefully tended sycamore groves, sculpted hedges, and budding rose gardens, the moonlight shone upon multi-acred estates, one after another, in a seemingly endless succession.

Beaver pulled into a wide paved drive, accented on either side by a massive stone lion, and drove slowly under the black star-studded sky, past the tennis courts and swimming pool, and came to a stop under a covered portico. Tumbling out of the jeep, the foursome made their way toward the Tudor mansion, feeling the effervescence of victory filling the air and bubbling from their surroundings.

Peter put an arm around Sally and drew her closer to his side. She smiled, feeling now as if it were the most natural movement in the world. Tonight she was Pete Decker's girl. Tonight. And that was all that mattered. A rich warmth filled her veins, her limbs, her spirit. She would not allow it to be marred by moments other than now.

"A penny for your thoughts?" Pete looked down into her eyes and focused on the pensive expression spreading across her lovely face.

"Sorry." She smiled, banishing her thoughts before he could read them. "They're not for sale. But everything's all right. Don't worry." She let her fingers slide between his as they walked through the silver shadows of the hedges. A warm breeze pressed against her, tossing her hair into spun flax. Together they made their way through the ever-increasing crowd milling in the main entryway

and moved on into a large walnut-paneled room. Royals'
memorabilia were scattered along the massive bookshelves
and a picture of the team hung above the mantel.

"I told you our host was quite a fan!" Pete whispered
to Sally and the two laughed lightly.

"P. J.! P. J. Decker! Gee, it's great to see you." A
vivacious blonde swept across the room and claimed
Pete's free arm. "Team parties just aren't the same without you, P. J.," she whined, her voice dripping with invitation.

"Ah, Jayne, yes, well . . ." P. J. took a step back. "Sally,
I'd like you to meet Jayne Cummings, a tried and true
Royals fan." Jayne giggled, at the same time giving Sally
the once-over. P. J. seemed not to notice and continued,
"Jayne hasn't missed a team party in five years, and I
think she even comes to one or two of the games!"

Again Jayne laughed, oblivious to his sarcasm, and
drew P. J. closer as her ample breasts, loosely encased in
a sheer, low-necked blouse, rubbed against his side.

P. J. winced as she applied unwanted pressure on his
injured shoulder. Sally immediately reacted. "It has been
very nice to meet you, Jayne. Oh, Pete, I think I see Joey
Rao over at the fireplace. Why don't we say hello?"

He nodded and led Sally away. "Pete?" The deserted
blonde mumbled under her breath. "She calls him Pete?"

"Well, if it isn't my favorite sportscaster!" Joey Rao
greeted Sally warmly and gave her a hug.

Sally couldn't repress the flush that rose immediately to
her cheeks. "Well, Joey, I'm afraid I'm taking a brief
sabbatical from the sports scene at present."

"Really? Why? We all thought you did a terrific job at
spring training."

Sally felt Pete's eyes upon her. "It seems they needed
someone to host a cooking show for a few months, and
since P. J. was available to help out in the sports depart-
ment . . ."

"Cooking show?" A petite olive-skinned woman standing on Joey's other side cut in to the conversation. "Well, you two certainly make an interesting team. P. J. is the one who taught me how to cook years ago." The attractive young woman smiled warmly into Sally's eyes. "P. J.'s terrific in the kitchen!"

"Yes, I know. He's already taught me a lot."

Peter cleared his throat with an exaggerated sound and Sally blushed, then cast him a silencing look.

The dark-haired woman laughed. "Since the men around here don't seem to pay much attention to formalities, let me introduce myself. I'm Gina Rao, and I'm awfully pleased to meet you, Sally. *And* I'm glad to know someone is watching out for P. J. while he's recuperating." She winked at Peter. "P. J., I think you're in good hands."

"You can bet your life on it!" Pete answered enthusiastically. "Sally is speeding up the healing process by a factor of ninety-nine!"

A look of friendly understanding passed between Gina and P. J. as the catcher's wife took Sally by the arm. "Come, Sally. I can see by the look in those baseball eyes that Joey and P. J. are about to launch into a boringly detailed analysis of the last seventeen plays of today's game. So, if you're not up to scrutinizing the exact curve of the pitcher's fingers or computing speed times distance, let me introduce you around."

Heads turned as the attractive duo, the lovely golden-haired woman and her striking black-haired counterpart, moved about the spacious room. Sally was immediately aware of the differing responses her presence evoked in the other guests: wives, team officials, players, guests. The players eyed her speculatively, appreciatively, as Gina made the introductions. The "flies," as the groupies were called by the wives, quickly took her measure, judged their competition, and were worried by what they saw. The wives themselves were cordial, but wary, as if afraid she were somehow intent on breaking into their closely knit circle.

"Don't mind them, Sally," Gina insisted after an especially cool response. "We players' wives are a special breed. We've earned our battle scars. The reserve comes from experience, a protection, I guess."

"Against what?" Sally was confused, lost in this suddenly alien world.

"Good question. I'm not sure I've got the answer, Sally. Against the outside world, I guess. We're not a big part of it, you see. But our men"—she cast a glance at the groups of players standing together, drinking, laughing, flirting with the many beautiful women flaunting their wares—"our men definitely *are!* And it takes a while to work all of that out. I guess the cliquishness is a protection of sorts." Gina smoothed the wrinkles from her forehead and smiled gently. "I don't mean to make it sound so mysterious and formidable, Sally. Those gals you just met are nice people, all of them. But they're reluctant to expose themselves to any degree. And you, and all the other females here,"—her graceful hand swept the room—"are outsiders, and a threat."

"But don't you get lonely, Gina?"

Gina laughed, a warm, bubbly sound. "Yes! Sometimes it is lonely. But just when it begins to get me down, I meet a nice person like you and realize that too much isolation is bad for the soul. So come now, tell me something about Sally Denning before I warp you completely against the family life of baseball folk! It's not so bad, you know. Especially when there's someone like Joey to welcome home after those long road trips and grueling games."

Sally saw the look of love, admiration, and fulfillment in Gina's eyes, and a shiver ran through her body. For a moment she was caught up in a fantasy of wrapping herself in Pete Decker's affection. Affection? Why could she never say "love," not even to herself? With a toss of her head she pushed away the thoughts and smiled back at Gina.

The two women continued across the room. "So, Sally, did I understand Joey correctly that your first love is sportscasting?"

Sally laughed. "Obsession is more like it. It's probably genetic. You see, my father is a sports hound from way back, and my brother was a baseball player. He was about to turn pro before Vietnam . . . changed all that."

"Oh, Sally, I'm sorry." Gina touched her on the arm, understanding the sorrow in her voice.

"After Matt died, I was the only one left. The only one to connect the Denning family with sports." Sally paused and shrugged her narrow shoulders. "And my father, he's seventy-nine now, is so proud of me! You'd think I was the all-star player rather than merely the reporter. He tells all his buddies at the rest home about his 'famous daughter'!" She chuckled softly. "It seems to mean a lot to him."

"I'm sure it does, Sally. And I'm certain you do a fine job." Her eyes probed the expression on Sally's face. Her voice dropped off. "Well, enough friendly prying. I'd like to make a stop in the powder room before we rejoin our men."

Sally followed Gina into a softly lit bedroom and let the door swing closed behind her. Several women sat on the edge of the wide bed chatting quietly, and another group sat perched before the mirrored vanity freshening their makeup. As Gina introduced her to the women, Sally realized they were all wives or fiancées of Royals players. She watched them with curiosity, recognizing the now-familiar coolness with which they greeted her, the careful scrutiny of her clothes, her hair, her figure. Gina was obviously a well-liked member of the group, and as she chatted in her effusive manner, the other women's aloofness began to fade, and Sally was slowly drawn into the conversation.

"So you're with P. J. tonight." Carole Owens, the striking brunette wife of the Royals' relief pitcher, made the statement in a way that demanded an explanation.

"Yes," Sally answered, "along with several others from the station. We've all been working together since Peter . . . P. J. joined our crew."

"Well, what do you think?" Another brunette joined the conversation.

"Oh, it's working out fine. P. J. is a great announcer and—"

"No, no! I mean, what do you think of our favorite playboy? We wives have all taken P. J. under our wings, and we keep tabs on what he's up to."

"I see . . . Well . . . I think he's very nice."

Carole Owens giggled. "Come on, Sally! We all know he's *nice*." She stretched out the word, giving it a distasteful sound. "What do you think about being among Decker's chosen? Keeping up with his affairs is more fun than following the latest soaps!"

Gina broke in. "Come on, girls. Give Sally a chance. She happens to be very nice—not at all like P. J.'s usuals. Besides, you're not being fair to Decker."

"You're probably right, Gina." Another wife responded, her voice soft. "Sorry, Sally. We're accustomed to a different breed at these parties. Did you notice all those 'flies' out there? We're used to having to shoo them away and, well, perhaps we were a bit out of line. But since you're here with P. J., that puts you in the spotlight automatically, as I'm sure you've noticed."

"Yes, I did notice," Sally answered defensively. "And I'm afraid I wasn't quite prepared for it. But believe me, I'm not a groupie and never, *ever* will be!"

The girls laughed and Sally settled into a chair near the bed. She should never have come here tonight. She had put herself in an unreal situation, an unreal world. Even worse, she had let herself get carried away by her own foolish dreams. She had never been able to cope with short-term relationships, yet maybe that was the only thing in the cards for her and Peter Decker. Maybe these other women were right. Maybe this relationship could be stretched only as long as the muscles in Pete's hurt shoulder. Once that wound healed, Pete would leave and her healing would have to begin. Could she handle that? Did she even want to try?

Another sharp voice interrupted her thoughts. "Sally, I must say, I for one am thrilled to see P. J. with someone like you." This came from the batting coach's wife. "Someone not out for a piece of the limelight, for a change."

Gina sat down next to Sally. "I agree. And I think she's already been a good influence on him."

"Well, Sally." Carole gave her a long, intense look. "God knows he needs it. But here's a little free advice. If you have any room left for decision, if you're not crazy in love with the guy, end it now and find yourself a nice, sane CPA, or a dentist or the like, and save yourself a lot of grief. This can be a crazy life."

Sally listened to the continuing banter, feeling the clash of the words as they bounced off her raw emotions. Crazy life. Playboy. Groupies.

Then a southern drawl crooned through the room. "But Gawd, aren't they just the sweetest boys on earth!"

There were murmurs of agreement, laughter, then Sally and Gina exited back to the crowded party room.

"Ah, there you are." Peter's deep voice caressed her. "I was afraid I had lost you for good." He ushered her into a quiet corner as Joey swept Gina onto the dance floor. "Where have you been, Cinderella? I was about to go looking for a glass slipper."

"I've been meeting the players' wives."

Pete groaned. "Oh, no. I should have warned you first.

133

But, Sally," he cautioned with a twinkle in his eye, "I'm sure with your reporter's training you can handle that with an objectivity far beyond the reach of mere mortals."

"Right." She laughed. "But I do think underneath all that armor they're really nice people, just caught up in a strange way of life. They did give me quite a candid view of the inner sanctum of a ball player's life."

"Oh?" Pete's brows shot up. "I thought I'd done that. You know you're welcome in *my* inner sanctum anytime." He flashed that look of hungry sensuality that she found so difficult to resist, sending waves of heat and desire through her limbs and down her spine. She felt her heart begin to race and fought for control.

"I've got to remember to be more specific with you, Decker. When will I ever learn! It was a candid view of a player's wife's life that they were very freely offering." Her voice was too high, too shrill.

Pete lifted his arm and wrapped it tightly over her shoulders. "Sally, don't be too taken in by what they've said." His voice was soft and husky. "It's different for every couple, you know. Just like in any relationship. It all depends on the two people involved, what each of them wants. You decide, then go for it."

Sally felt herself stiffen. "That simple, huh? And do you always *get* it?" Her voice was demanding now.

"Hey, calm down." He kissed her lightly, brushing her hair back with the tips of her fingers. "What's the matter, Sally? I didn't mean to make you bristle. Is something troubling you, sweetheart?" His voice was warm and caring, and Sally recognized the honest concern in his words, but she didn't want him to be concerned. Suddenly she needed space. Time.

Peter looked at her in puzzlement. "Sally, what *is* bothering you? Tell me."

Sally laughed lightly, not trusting a serious tone.

"Nothing. Nothing at all. This is a terrific party. And I'd love to dance, but first I need to powder my nose. I'll meet you at the dance floor." She smiled brightly and disappeared across the room.

Sally looked at herself in the wide mirror and lightly dusted powder across her high cheekbones. *Okay, Sally Denning, go out there and have fun. Peter Decker is a great man. Enjoy him! Stop expecting so much from yourself and everyone around you!* With forced determination she pushed open the door and stepped back into the crowded room.

"Hey, there she is!" A loud, slurred voice stopped her, and she found herself flanked by two towering figures. She immediately recognized Dave Owens, the relief pitcher, and the other was an outfielder whose name she had forgotten.

"Hey, beautiful, ever since spring training we've all been wanting to get to know you better. And now to find out Decker beat us to the punch, as usual!"

"Oh! So *you're* Decker's newest dolly! Small world."

Sally cringed at the words. For a brief moment she wanted to flee, to run, to leave the party far behind her. Silly! She calmed herself. They've just had a little too much to drink, that's all. She reminded herself that she had grown up with baseball players, and she certainly hadn't been afraid of these same men a few short weeks ago when she crashed into their own dressing room! "Small world it is, fellows. Now, if you'll excuse me."

"Hey, wait!" A third voice joined the group. "You guys are hogging all the action. Someone introduce me to Decker's delightful date here. You know P. J., he's always willing to share."

"And with his abundance of babes," retorted the outfielder above the heavy male laughter, "he can well afford to!"

135

Sally angrily pushed her way past the barricade of broad shoulders and found herself face to face with Gina.

"You okay, Sally?" Gina cast an angry glance from one player to the next. "You guys better cool it. This isn't a high school dance, you know!" She glanced quickly at Sally as they escaped the raucous group. "Pay them no mind, Sally."

Sally forced a smile. "I know they're just wound up after the big victory. No problem, Gina . . ." Her voice trailed off. She found Peter right where he said he'd be. She saw the outline of his back as he stood, one hand thrust in his pocket, his legs slightly apart. Every fiber of her being wanted to reach out and grab him, press him close to her, hold him tight. Her arms could feel his warmth, her lips taste his kisses. But her mind could only register the players' innuendos, the wives' warnings, her own fears and insecurities. Absentmindedly she reached out and patted Gina on the arm, thanking her and bidding her good night, then took three quick steps that brought her to Pete's side.

"Hi!" she managed brightly. "There's been a slight change in plans. I'm leaving now. Beaver has to get back to Lawrence. He has an early video tomorrow morning and I'm going to ride back with him."

"But I told you I'd drive you back, Sally." His voice was firm, warning.

"Yes, I know, Decker, but that's silly. It's so far out of your way. And besides, I'm tired, too, and ready to leave."

"There it is again. We're back to Decker! Okay, Sally. What is it this time? You seem to have a definite allergic reaction to parties, at least ones which I also attend. You've done this to me before, you know." His eyes were accusing, puzzled, and Sally could see the hurt within.

"I . . . I'm sorry."

"All right, Sally." Pete's voice grew soft and husky as he scanned her face. "I won't try to stop you. I won't try to force you to explain. But the prince will pick up the glass slipper just so many times, Sally. Remember that. One of these nights it's going to break." He drew her close for a brief moment, kissed her tenderly on the lips, and murmured against her, "I just don't understand how you find it so easy to leave me." Then he disappeared into the crowd.

CHAPTER SEVEN

Waves of humid summer heat settled heavily upon Lawrence, Kansas, and the hum of air conditioners filled the studios of WQEK. Summer also brought out skeleton crews, altered schedules for vacationing staff, and a slower pace as reruns received top priority in program scheduling.

But Sally Denning was oblivious to the slowdown; she attacked her cooking show with a vengeance. She slipped into the studios with the earliest security guard and didn't leave until the city was blanketed with darkness.

"Sally, this is ridiculous!" Robin chastised her friend one sultry Friday morning. "You don't even take time for breakfast."

Sally laughed and lifted her lithe frame onto one of the studio stools. "It's my heat-wave remedy, Robin. The studio is like a space lab—cool, controlled, isolated—and if I get here early enough, I can avoid the stifling suffering of the rest of humanity here in my little cocoon."

"And you're happy as a clam, right?" Robin eyed her friend with a knowing look. "Sal, I don't mean to interfere, but I've watched you dart around corners for days.

138

You sneak in and out of the building at god-awful hours and jump at the sound of a certain voice from two rooms down the hall. Well, it's obvious you're either wanted by the FBI or trying desperately to avoid that certain someone."

The past days *had* been uncomfortable, but Sally had managed to put distance between herself and Pete, and she needed to keep it there. She had managed to run into him only in crowded places and had been only cordial, impersonal. As for Peter he'd fix her with an indecipherable look, a teasing smile, and go on his way. The last couple of days she had become so adept as not to see him at all. She felt the deflated sense of unwanted success, but knew that was the way it had to be. It was better for both herself *and* Peter, she sagely advised. Solves the problem of inevitable tearful farewells, and God knows what else.

She shuddered slightly, then plucked an apron off a hook and threw it at Robin. "The only avoidance around here is of *work!* Come on, Producer. I need your help in preparing this lamb. Young and milk-fed. Just what the doctor ordered."

Robin stood and allowed the moment to pass. She knew Sally well enough not to pursue a subject once that curtain had been drawn behind Sally's eyes. Accepting the proffered apron, she stepped behind the counter. "Okay, chef, mutton it is."

Later that evening Sally walked through the nearly deserted halls and rode the quiet elevator down to the lobby. She was bone tired, and luxuriated in a series of long, stretching yawns. She and Robin had put together another smashing show and Sally was quietly pleased.

She had, through long hours and patient diligence, guided her viewers—and herself—through the beginning steps of cooking and on to planning their first elegant dinner party. The viewers loved her, laughed with her, learned with her. And Sally found herself actually enjoying the broadcasts. She even accepted an invitation to write an article for the local Sunday magazine on how to conquer cooking. She rediscovered satisfaction in the flow of words from mind to paper. Yes, writing was a release—even about cooking fears if not doubleheaders. She'd have to remember that.

Pushing open the heavy double doors, Sally stepped out into the blackness. A northern breeze had blown across the city in the evening hours, giving a brief respite from the haze of heat. Sally took a deep breath and looked up into the clear sky. The gnarled, fully leafed branches of the maples and oaks met above her head, creating intricate patterns against the darkness. Leaning back against the front of the building, Sally stood beneath the vast ceiling and watched the drama unfold above her. A lone cloud floated in front of the crescent moon; a flash of light caught her attention and she glimpsed the tail of a falling star before it disappeared billions of light-years away.

If only life here were like that, she thought. Ordered. Beautiful. Predictable. Lovely and remote. *It would be easy to live like that, I think.* Crickets rubbed their legs in the nearby grass, singing nature's simple harmonies, and Sally found herself slipping into a wonderful state of detachment. Then a bright twinkle between the tree branches caught her attention. The old habit overtook her, and she closed her eyes, tilted her chin, and began to wish on the first star.

"I wish I may, I wish I might . . ." Beaver's deep voice broke the hush, surprising her in the darkness.

"Oh, Beaver! You startled me."

"Sorry, Sally." He smiled down at her. "Do you think you'll get your wish?"

"Oh, Beaver, it gets hard to know *what* to wish. Maybe just that things will turn out well in the end for everyone."

"It takes more than wishes, Sally." He gave her a long,

brotherly look. "By the way, did you know Decker has been gone for a few days? You hadn't asked."

Sally swallowed, her throat suddenly dry. "Where has he gone?"

"I don't know, Sally. I just overheard Slater saying P. J. was having some trouble with his shoulder and would be out for a while."

Something was wrong with Peter. Her detachment shattered into pieces at her feet. She gave Beaver a quick, impulsive hug. "Thank you, Beaver. Thank you for telling me."

The moment the alarm sounded the next morning, Sally tossed off the light sheet that was her only covering, slipped into a pair of shorts and T-shirt, and headed for Kansas City. She didn't stop for coffee. Didn't stop to think. If she did, she knew she'd be lost. This roller-coaster ride with Decker had her worn thin. It had to stop. Yet each time the ride seemed over, there she was again, buying another ticket. The memories of those untraveled, dizzying heights drew her back. That soaring ecstasy at the touch of his hand. The love she felt for him. But no, she insisted, her voice loud with emphasis in the little car, this time it's different. This time I'm going as a friend, as someone who cares. If what Beaver said was true, Peter would need someone, and she wouldn't desert him.

The gatekeeper waved her on with a smile and she parked in front of the house and rang the bell. At first there was no answer, then Sally heard footsteps and the door swung open.

"Yes? May I help you?" An older woman, her hair flecked with gray, stood just within.

"Yes, please," Sally covered her surprise. "I was hoping to see Mr. Decker."

"I'm sorry. Mr. Decker is not available at the moment,"

141

the woman answered with ease born of long practice. "If you would care to leave a message?"

"Of course. My name is Sally Denning, and—"

"*You're* Sally Denning? Why didn't you say so, dearie. Now just you step right along in here."

"But you said—"

"No buts about it! You're just the medicine he needs. Wait here for a short minute." She held a quieting finger to her lips and pushed a button on the intercom. "Mr. Decker?"

There was a momentary buzz of static, then Pete's voice. "Yes, Ella?"

"There is someone to see you, sir."

"I'm not . . . Ow, hold it a minute, would ya, Steve? . . . I'm sorry, Ella. I thought you understood I wasn't seeing anyone."

"But, sir, it's Sally Denning."

"Sally?" There was a long pause, and then his voice again, filled with barely controlled excitement. "Ella, if you're putting me on . . ."

The housekeeper beckoned Sally closer, then nodded encouragingly.

Sally, blushing under her tan, spoke softly into the intercom. "Peter?"

"Sally soufflé! Hooray for my team! Come on down, baby."

Sally dashed down the steps to the basement. What had she done to deserve such a welcome? She drew to a shy halt at the bottom of the stairs. "Hi, Pete."

He was lying on his stomach on the top of a flat massage table halfway across the room. The room itself was a gym as fully equipped as any in the health spas she had frequented. Weight stations, Nautilus equipment, mats, exercise bars, massage tables, a whirlpool, and a sauna. Sally took a quick look around and whistled.

"Whew! You've got enough equipment for Mr. America!"

"Hello, Sally." Pete grinned, his brown eyes sparkling with warmth. "But, honey, I thought that's who I was!"

She took a step closer and Peter held out his hand. Sally hesitated. "I wasn't sure you'd be very happy to see me. I thought . . ."

"Hush, baby. You came when I needed you."

"But, Pete, you didn't even tell me. What if I hadn't found out?"

"That thought occurred to me, what with that fancy two-step you'd been doing to avoid me. But I knew if you cared, you'd find out. You'd miss me, even if you didn't want to. I knew you'd come. And I just couldn't ask again. You had to come to *me.*" His fingers stretched wide, reaching for her, and she slipped her hand into his. He smiled, with a quiet, sure joy. "You know, a man can bend only so far before he breaks. *I've* got some pride too."

"Not a hell of a lot, lookin' at you now, fella!" A deep male voice interrupted.

Sally jumped, but Pete only laughed and tightened his hold on her fingers.

"Forgot you were there, Steven! Well, come on over and meet my girl. Sally, this is my own personal Attila the Hun. Tortures me, the man does! but really, he's the best PT in the business. Steve Wyatt, meet Sally Denning."

"Real nice to meet you, ma'am."

Her hand was swallowed up in an enormous palm. Then that same palm smacked resoundingly on Pete's flank. "Ha! You're lucky to have me, P. J. I'm the best thing that ever happened to you." He winked over Pete's bare torso at Sally. "Until now, that is."

"Nice to meet you too, Steve." The blood was high in her cheeks. The intrusion of a stranger had made her acutely uncomfortable. Here she was in this very male setting alone with two men—one a near giant, the other

143

near naked. In fact, all that covered Pete was a small towel across his rump. His chin was propped on his good hand, and the muscles on his shoulders were bunched and knotted as he leaned up to look at her.

"Well, P. J. What do ya say? Want to call the session off, now that you've got company?"

P. J.'s brow wrinkled in indecision. He looked from Sally back over his shoulder to Steve. "I don't know. What do you think? Can I afford to miss a day?"

The therapist shrugged. "Up to you, man. Depends if you want to play again this season."

Pete glared at him with more anger than Sally had ever seen in his eyes before. "And what the hell's *that* supposed to mean?"

"You asked."

"Not for a put-down!"

"Sorry, P. J. I guess it surprised me that you even had to ask. But the answer is 'no.' You can't afford to miss a session."

"Sally?" P. J. turned to her.

Sally stepped closer and trailed a hand over P. J.'s cheek. "I'm glad I came, but don't let me interrupt. Now that I know you're okay, and Ella's here to get what you need, I'll come back another time."

"No, I don't want you to leave." There was an unexpected urgency in his voice. "Do you mind waiting? Just keep us company, would you, Sally?"

"Yeah, Sally. Please stay. Hopefully your presence will stifle his curses. My ears are ringing!"

Sally nodded, laughing. "Sure, Steve. I'll protect you."

P. J. turned his face until his lips rested against her palm. Then he let go of her hand. "Okay, Attila, go to it!"

Sally sank down on one of the mats, leaned comfortably against the wall, and watched.

Steve began to work on Pete's good side, his huge hands kneading, pulling, probing, stretching. He worked the muscles and tendons, strengthening the ligaments, loosening the joints. Sally watched as he lifted Pete's throwing arm off the table and worked on it with careful attention. From across the room she could hear Pete's grunts and groans as the huge hands worked on him. Then the hands moved on across his shoulders and neck, the wide span of his back. The fingers dug into the tanned flesh, leaving white pressure spots that slowly reddened. Steve reached down under the table, lifted a bottle, and splashed some oil on Pete's back. She could hear the sharp intake of his breath as the cold oil hit his sensitized skin, then the groan of pleasure as Steve massaged his back, rubbing, pounding, kneading. Steve circled the table, coming to stand on Pete's injured side, partially blocking her view.

"Sally? You're not too bored, are you? Would you like something to drink?" Pete asked in the brief lull.

"I'm fine, don't worry about me."

"But I do, darlin'. I do."

Then the smack of hands on flesh changed his gentle words to a grunt. "Easy, Steve! Take it easy on that side, would you?"

Again the wide hands began to probe, massage, lifting the hurt shoulder from the table to rub and knead the unused muscles. Beads of sweat stood out on Pete's brow and across his upper lip. His hand clenched tight in pain, the nails digging into his palm as Steve worked on down the hurt arm.

Sally felt her own stomach tighten, twisting painfully. She could feel the sharp stabs of pain, the soreness of the tender muscles.

A moan escaped the white, set line of Pete's lips. He turned his face away from her.

Steve manipulated the weak shoulder. He stretched the arm out wide. Then, keeping the elbow straight, he lifted it up over Peter's head.

Sally heard his soft words of encouragement, the shal-

145

lowness of Peter's breathing, and his groans as muscles strained for forgotten suppleness. The sweat ran freely down Peter's side, soaking the towel beneath him. His hair clung damply to the back of his neck.

"Enough, Steve, enough!" he muttered through clenched teeth.

"Almost got it, boy. Come on. Another stretch and—"

"I said enough!"

"And I said, *no!* I'm the boss down here, and I say we go for it again." Without waiting for a reply, he began again to loosen, then stretch the tight shoulder.

This time Sally had to close her eyes to keep from crying out. She couldn't bear to see Peter in so much pain. She just couldn't stand it.

Peter himself had gone pale beneath his tan. The sweat glistened on his body.

"Got it!" Steve's voice was triumphant. "Look at that, P. J. Straight as an arrow! Now roll it, kid. See if you can use that shoulder."

Pete's hands circled once slowly, then again, more smoothly.

With an exultant cry he rolled onto his back. "See that, Sally! Did you see that, baby? It's going to be all right!"

Sally flew to his side. "I saw! You were great! You *are* the greatest!"

"Now hold on." He reached lovingly for her cheek. "Got to give a little credit to this fellow here." He grinned over at Steve.

"Oh, I do. I do! You're great too, Steve. Although if I had gotten my hands on you a few moments ago I could have killed you."

"Well, let's not dwell on the past, Ms. Denning. Here, you can put your hands to good use now." He took hold of Sally's wrists and pressed her hands against Pete's chest. "Now I'm going to call it a day, but this boy could use a little mellowing. That bottle there's full of oil. Just squirt a bit on and give him a good rubdown. He'll thank you for it later!"

With a light punch on Pete's good shoulder he turned and left.

The room filled with silence. Sally bent over and laid her face against Pete's cheek. He reached up and ruffled her hair, then whispered, "What do you say, Sally? Willing to give me a rubdown?"

"My pleasure, but I'm not sure I'm very good at this."

"Don't worry. I'll let you know if you do anything wrong." His hands circled around her head, drawing her face to his.

His kiss was sweet and lingering, an unhurried caress.

"First, honey, why don't you hand me a towel from underneath this thing." He mopped his chest and throat, and rubbed the terry over his hair, then pillowed it beneath his neck. "Okay." He grinned, securing the other towel more tightly about his hips. "Ready when you are."

Sally splashed the oil on his chest, giggling as he winced at its chill, then gently rubbed the heel of her palms against his skin. She trailed her fingers over the curves and planes of his muscles, across his chest, his ribs, the flat arc of his belly.

"Doin' fine, Sally. Doin' fine."

She grinned, embarrassed yet excited by their somewhat reversed roles. He, lying still and passive beneath her hands; she, free to savor the sensations flowing through her fingertips.

She stroked him lovingly, running her fingers through the curly hairs on his chest, over the pale outline of his hurt shoulder.

"It's okay, baby. You can press harder than that."

"I'm just afraid I'll hurt you."

"There's only one way you can hurt me, Sally."

"Oh, Peter." She leaned down to kiss him and suddenly

147

she was on top of him, the thin cotton of her shorts and T-shirt the only thing between his burning flesh and hers.

His kiss had the lick of fire, setting her ablaze, lips to toes, tingling, aching.

With a laugh that rumbled deep within his chest, Pete rolled onto his side, hugging her tight. The towel fell away and Sally felt him move against her. His eyes smiled into hers, and he dusted her face with kisses. "Oh, Sally soufflé, let me love you—let me, baby."

"We'll both fall off and kill ourselves, Pete Decker! I can just see it in the paper now: SPORTS HERO PLUNGES TO DEATH FROM MASSAGE TABLE!"

He roared with laughter. Then he slapped her smartly on the rump; the sting sent her jumping from the table. "Hey, watch it, fella!"

Pete winked. "You've just given me a better idea. Follow me, madam."

He slowly eased his richly muscled body off the table, strode across the room, and turned on the jets in the whirlpool. With a roguish grin he beckoned her to him.

Sally took a step closer, then stopped. She peeked at him from beneath lowered lids, her face turned coyly away. "And just what do you have in mind, Decker?"

"In mind? It wasn't my mind doing the prompting. I'd say this little idea came from somewhere else. Let's call it a 'gut reaction.'" He winked, rubbing his palm across his belly. He lowered himself into the tub, holding onto the side with his good hand. His hair fell across his eyes and he tossed his head back and smiled up at her. The white edge of his teeth showed through his parted lips. His dimple deepened in a semblance of innocence. "Well, Sally, do you have any idea how therapeutic a whirlpool can be, especially when shared?"

Sally walked over, reached down, and brushed the hair off his forehead. "No, Mr. Decker. I'm afraid I haven't had your wide range of experience."

148

"Ah, that's all right, Sally soufflé." His strong features softened with gentleness. "I'm as good a coach as I am a player." He reached up and brushed his forefinger across her lips. "Come on down with me, baby."

"Well, I just don't know. What if Steve or Ella comes down?"

"Nobody comes down uninvited."

"But what if—"

"What if you just stop worrying, okay?" And with a flash of his hand he reached into the water and twisted the jet. A white spurt of water cut the surface, breaking into a froth of bubbles as it drenched the front of her, knees to shoulder.

"Decker, you nut!" she yelped, shielding her breasts with open hands. But her heart raced wildly.

"Here you go, Sally!" He caught her arm in a firm grasp and pulled her down across his lap. The water splashed down over the sides and gurgled in the drains, but their lusty laughter muffled the sounds.

Sally felt the heat of the water as it saturated her clothes. Then Pete's hands slipped beneath them, drew them off, and there was only the water and him. She felt the warm, rushing embrace of the bath, the swirling tingle of the moving water, the power of Pete's arms, his mouth on hers.

"Ummmm, the fans are cheering, the pitcher's on the mound . . ." he teased against her lips.

Their fingers met, entwined, then separated, tracing separate but parallel paths across each other's bodies.

"The pitch is away . . ." Pete whispered, his breathing fast and shallow.

She felt his hands wash across her back and hips, flowing across her stomach and between her thighs. His flesh echoed her response as she touched and stroked him, all the while murmuring soft love words.

"And the crowd is going wild . . ." Pete's chest rose and

fell in ragged breaths. His mouth moved hard against hers. His hands touched her. The blood in her veins surged and ebbed as his fingers worked their magic. Her voice was a whisper of pleasure in a whirlpool of passion. She held fast to him, his body the rock to which she clung.

"Oh, Sally, Sally," he moaned, straining beneath her hands.

She felt heated streams of water, but could no longer tell whether they were within or without. Her body melted; her sweetness diffused, dissolved. Her pulse beat heavily deep within her. Her being centered there. All else was fluid, floating. Then Pete caught her lips between his, his hands tightening across her back. She felt him surge and slide within her and the river of her blood became a torrent. She held him, as his strength filled her. The waters gathered at the cliff's edge, gushing, swirling, surging, until in a wild joyous leap she plunged on over the edge and down in a flashing cascade of fulfillment.

Peter was there to catch her. Slowly her body took form again, molded by the touch of his hand. "Oh, Sally, Sally," he whispered sensuously. "I can't believe you're here with me."

CHAPTER EIGHT

The whirring of a motorboat and soft lapping of the waves in the distance stirred the early morning air. Sally slowly moved her slender body to wakefulness in the wide four-poster bed. Raising her thick lashes, she rolled over onto her side and felt the empty space beside her.

"Peter?" For a brief moment she was puzzled, unsure of her surroundings, certain only of the man who belonged beside her on the cool cotton sheets. "Pete?" Her eyes were wide open now, roaming lazily about the spacious room. The sheet fell down around her waist as she moved and the morning sunlight washed over her smooth skin, the shadows playing beneath her firm, rounded breasts.

In a moment Peter appeared in the doorway, a light robe covering his lean, hard frame. He bowed slightly and a playful smile curved his lips as he drank in the sight before him. Between his hands he balanced a large, rattan bed tray. "Madam," he murmured, his eyes caressing her soft skin, "breakfast is served." In a few long strides he was at the bedside, placing the tray carefully on a small table. He slipped his long body down beside Sally's.

On the tray a glass vase held two perfect roses, their

stems intertwined in the slender cylinder. Beneath misted glass domes were golden eggs Benedict, the creamy hollandaise sauce dripping down the muffins' crisp sides. Goblets of freshly squeezed orange juice were beside two large mugs of hot coffee. To the side was a large bowl of fruit, the orange and red slivers shining in the sunlight pouring in through the open window. Sally eyed the tray in amusement. "Peter," she said, her eyes twinkling, "Egg McMuffin . . . You shouldn't have!"

Slowly, Pete turned his body to face her, looking at her silently through hooded lids. Then in one swift movement he reached over, removed an ice cube from the bowl of chilled fruit, and slid it smoothly down the cleavage between her bare breasts until it rested between her legs. She bolted upright, her piercing cry echoing across the room. Through spurts of laughter she tugged at him, until the two collapsed amidst the tangled sheets.

"Good morning, my Sally soufflé." Pete's voice was husky as he muffled her laughter with his lips, covering her mouth, feeling the wet softness of her lips as he probed gently between them with the tip of his tongue. The sudden chill was completely forgotten as Sally responded immediately to the warmth of his touch. She reached inside his robe and pulled him to her, rubbing her fingers along the smoothness of his back and over the firm outline of his thighs. They fell back against the pillows, molding their bodies together. Sally felt the rush of blood flow through her veins, the heightened awareness of his strength as he pressed against her, the loss of all control as she floated with him, their fingers touching, exploring, gently caressing, tenderly.

"Oh, darling," Peter murmured as he slid his body over hers, feeling the response of her beneath him.

Sally felt herself rise, felt the boundaries of her body fall away as she soared again into the misty heights of fulfillment. For a long time she lay still in Pete's protective embrace, his legs entwined with hers, his fingers gently stroking her hair.

"Hmmmm," he murmured softly, "much better than eggs any day."

She watched him, his eyes closed, a lovely smile etched into his strong face. A lock of dark hair curled down near one eye, clinging to his forehead in its own pool of dampness. Sally reached over and brushed it back, letting her fingers linger on the side of his cheek. She moved her hand down, tracing the outline of his lips. They moved under her gentle pressure and nipped at her fingertips, teasing, inviting. Slowly Peter opened his eyes.

"You better watch it or I'll never give you another chance to taste my muffins."

"Oh?" Sally cocked one brow. "And I thought I already had!"

They laughed together in the luxurious afterglow of lovemaking when words and smiles need not make sense. They need only be shared.

Peter raised himself up on his strong elbow as Sally struggled to glimpse the small alarm clock beside the bed.

"Oh, no! No work today. It's Sunday, my sweet. All day long."

Sally sat upright. "Sunday! That's right! My visit to Pop. Oh, Pete, at the risk of ruining your beautiful breakfast, I'm going to have to eat quickly and run." She frowned, caught in the limbo between their passion and the day's demands. "That sounds awful, doesn't it!"

He looked at her with eyes still filled with need, then said with a smile in his voice, "Well, I have to admit, I could have come up with a better comment. It *was* a beautiful night, you know."

Sally's eyes misted. "Yes, that it was."

"And beautiful nights breed beautiful days. An old sailor's proverb, Sally." Peter ran his fingertips down the length of her back and over the gentle slope of her hips.

153

"And you know what they say about beautiful days, don't you?"

Sally's voice caught at the seriousness in his voice. She tried to put lightness in her voice when she replied. "Another proverb? No, what do they say?"

"Beautiful days breed beautiful lives."

His eyes searched hers but Sally tried to look beyond the gaze. She wanted to crawl inside of him, wanted to understand every inch of him. Don't talk to me in proverbs and riddles, Peter Decker, she pleaded silently. I think I love you.

Peter watched her carefully, then kissed her softly on the lips. "Come back, my Sal. My video is clouding over, slight snow on the screen."

"I'm right here." Then in an effort to mask her thoughts she grabbed a shirt from the end of the bed, slipped into it quickly, and exclaimed, "And I'm starved! These eggs Benedict will be ruined if we don't eat them soon!" With a playful tug she brought Peter to a sitting position beside her and the two dug into the carefully prepared, slightly cooled feast.

Pete insisted on driving Sally's small car. Under doctor's orders he needed the shoulder exercise. Sally settled back on the passenger side, grateful for the distance, and happy that Peter had something to devote his attention to besides herself. She had wanted to make the trip out to Twin Elms by herself. She had wanted to drive alone and have the chance to send all her confused emotions flying on the wind.

But Peter had been adamant. He refused even to consider an alternative, reminding her of how much Lou had enjoyed his last visit and all their sports talk. And, he added, sealing the decision, he had a genuine affection for the old man with his lively wit and homey ways.

Sally had acquiesced, reluctantly, knowing it would mean a lot to her father to have Peter there. He had rekindled a spark in Lou Denning's eyes she hadn't seen in years. But it created a link that Sally wasn't sure she wanted to cope with. The bond between Pete and her father could be broken so quickly, and so painfully. She knew she had given herself to him too quickly these past months, but she found herself becoming increasingly helpless. Unable to prevent him from manipulating her emotions and her thoughts, she was honestly no longer sure if she truly did want to prevent it. So she gave in, and made herself vulnerable. She only hoped that she would soon be able to slip out unscathed.

The giant sycamores made a canopy over the old country road. Sally leaned back, letting the sunlight flood her face, and breathed in the summer smells of wildflowers and corn husks waving with the golden wheat. Pete whistled contentedly as he guided the car over the one-lane bridges and through the open fields. She smiled at the tunes that wafted on the breeze and circled about her. He seemed to sense her need to be alone with her thoughts and, although Sally knew he cast frequent glances her way, allowed her that freedom.

"It's that next road to the right." Sally broke the silence with directions to the nursing home.

"Thanks, Sal. I remember. I bet Lou is on the front porch right now looking for a glimpse of red through the trees."

"Right." Sally laughed. "That's exactly where I usually find him, although occasionally he dozes off and forgets . . ." Her voice trailed off as the car pulled onto the winding gravel road leading up to the main building, and Sally felt the stirrings within her that preceded each visit to her aging father. She never knew quite how to label them—excitement, fear, anticipation—but they were always there, always coloring her thoughts.

Peter pulled into a parking place and Sally scanned the groups of old folk gathering on the lawn and wide porches.

She couldn't spot Lou although several of his friends waved warmly in welcome.

"Guess he's still at the cottage." Sally headed down the familiar walk and Pete fell in beside her, matching her stride.

The door flung open as they neared the small cabin and Gus Lindstrom strode out onto the steps. He gathered Sally into a welcoming hug, then stood back a step before he spoke.

"Sally! So glad you could make it today. It will really pep the old geezer up. And P. J., Lou hasn't stopped talking about your visit yet! This'll be great, just great."

"Where is Pop, Gus? Is he still sleeping?" Her voice was hesitant, tinged suddenly with an unknown fear.

"I dunno, Sally. He was awake an hour or so ago when I went up to see him."

"Went up where? Where is he, Gus?" Now Sally's fear was open and acknowledged. "What has happened." She jerked the old man's arm, her eyes open wide.

"Hey, Sally, Lou is fine. You calm down now. Just a little bump on his head, that's all. But he's fine."

"A bump on his head? What happened, Gus?"

The white-haired man wrapped his gnarled fingers around Sally's hands. "Now, calm down, darlin'. Everything is going to be all right. I thought they had called you yesterday when it happened. They said they were goin' to."

Sally's eyes clouded. There wasn't any way anyone could have gotten hold of her yesterday, unless they had a private line to Peter's whirlpool or bed. Her face flooded with shame and guilt, but the old man continued.

"Anyway, really doesn't matter because Lou is going to be just fine. Can't keep a good man down, doncha know, Sal. So come on, you and your nice friend here, and we'll go on up to the big house and brighten up Lou's day."

Sally allowed the men to lead her up to the main house

156

where the infirm residents were cared for. Her mind was racing with foggy thoughts and unexplained details as she struggled to calm herself.

"How did he hurt himself, Gus?" The three walked through the wide doors and into the lobby of the home.

"Well"—Gus chuckled softly—"I think it was one of his sly efforts to escape an afternoon with Wanda Olfant. I saw him slip around the corner of the porch heading for the back stairs, just as the old biddy called out his name. She has the hots for him, you know."

Sally managed a thin smile.

"Anyway, Lou must have slipped on that step, skidded to the bottom, and knocked his head on the post as he tried to break his fall. Had quite a headache and some dandy bruises, but other than that the doc says he'll be fine in no time, fit as a fiddle." Gus led them down a quiet, carpeted hallway with small rooms off to either side and a medicinal odor in the air. In the middle of the hall was a large desk with a uniformed nurse behind it.

"Hi, Gustave!" She called brightly. "And you must be Sally Denning. Lou has been asking for you." She smiled, then looked at Peter, a questioning look on her face. "And you . . . are P. J. Decker!" Recognition flooded her face as she beamed at the famous ball player. "We heard you were here once before and those of us off duty were furious. But no one expected you back!"

Pete's husky voice filled the hallway. "We came to see Lou. How is he?" He sensed Sally's unease and quickly turned the conversation back to her. "Sally would like to see him now, if that's okay."

"Yes, yes, of course." The nurse turned her attention to Sally and Gus. "But, Ms. Denning, it might be better if you could wait a short while. The doctor just gave him a shot and I'm afraid he'll be a little woozy for a while. In fact, here's Dr. Anderson right now. Why don't you talk to him?" The nurse led Sally and Gus to a small alcove off the hallway where she quickly introduced her to Lou's doctor. Pete moved a discreet distance down the hallway to allow them some privacy. As he headed toward a chair in a waiting area, he heard Lou's familiar voice coming out of a nearby room.

"Nurse . . . nurse . . . Sally? Sally, are you out there?" His words were slurred and weak. Peter looked over to the group in the alcove but they were deep in conversation. Again Lou's voice filtered through the hall and Peter moved quickly toward the sound. He was drawn into a small, sun-drenched room; a neat dresser and chair lined one wall, facing a hospital bed on the other. Lou Denning was leaning back in bed, his bandaged head resting on a mound of white pillows. He struggled to sit upright as Peter approached, then collapsed back against the sea of white. A soft glaze covered his eyes and he examined Peter with a faraway look, a peculiar smile curving his thin lips.

"Matt . . ." His voice was strained and drowsy. "Matt, it is you, isn't it?" Tears sprung to the old man's eyes as he held out his hands, beckoning Peter closer. "My son, come closer." Peter hesitated for a moment, wincing at the hope that shone in the old man's tired eyes and the love that sang in his words. Again the old man struggled toward his visitor.

Peter moved closer, fearful that Lou would strain himself. "Lou, it's P. J. Decker, Sally's friend."

But again he heard the old man mumble, "Matt, our Matt. Best damned third baseman in the Midwest."

A muffled sob caused Peter to turn. Sally stood outlined in the doorway, her hands pressed to her face, her eyes wide with pain. As Peter took a step toward her, he recognized something else. Mixed in with the pain was anger and distance and a look he had never seen in her eyes before. He stopped and watched as she brushed past him and leaned over her father.

"Pop, it's me, Sally. How are you?" Her voice was low

and soothing. "That's quite an egg you have there." Gently, Sally fingered the bandage on his forehead, her eyes moist.

"Sally. Well, goodness me, about time you got here!" His voice strengthened and Pete could hear it clear as the fog seemed to pass. "Sally, Sally, sure am glad to see you. Doctors tried to get you yesterday but you weren't home but don't you worry. Takes more than a flight of stairs to keep Lou Denning down. Just like my kids." His voice drifted again and his eyes lost their focus. "Yep, my Sal. Keeps sportscasting clean and what it should be. And Matt . . . Matt . . . best damned third baseman I ever watched play. He'll keep the league goin' . . . yep . . . Matt . . ." Sally rested a cool hand on his head, urging him to rest.

She felt Peter's presence behind her. Slowly she turned. "Please go. You don't belong here." Her voice was unyielding, cold. "I want to be alone with my father."

"Sally, please . . ."

"No. Go, Peter."

He turned and slipped out of the room; his departure allowed Sally to release the tears she had been holding on to tightly. She turned back toward Lou, but the medicine had finally taken its toll and his eyes were closed, his breathing deep and somnolent. She cried softly and painfully, cursing porch stairs, broadcasting, sports, and P. J. Decker. The emotions swirled before her, then stretched out in an angry collage. One by one she tried to examine them, hoping to rid herself of the cruel confusion that shrouded her mind. But as hard as she tried what seemed like a permanent fog settled softly over her, trapping her in its haze.

Several hours later the nurse appeared at the door. "Ms. Denning, I think perhaps you had better leave now. Your father is going to be just fine but the best thing for him is rest."

Sally sat back in the chair and looked from the nurse to her father, then back to the nurse. "Yes, I'm sure you're right."

"Why don't you call Lou in the morning? He'll be much more alert then and I'm sure very anxious to talk to you."

Sally kissed her father gently on the forehead, thanked the nurse, and walked slowly out to her car. With each step unwanted images veiled the walkway in the hazy twilight. Matt Denning standing on a baseball diamond, her father in the front-row seat, Sally at the sportscaster's microphone announcing the day's action. Lou was beaming, supported by his loving pride. And then Pete Decker's face appeared and Sally moaned, feeling the tangled emotions begin to close in upon her. She felt exhausted, defeated. Somehow, deep down, she thought of Peter as the source of all the pain she now felt.

As she neared the parking lot she saw a lone figure silhouetted against the darkening sky. Peter leaned quietly against the hood of the car, waiting. Sally shuddered, brushed past him, and slid behind the wheel. As he settled himself in the seat beside her, she turned the keys quickly in the ignition and sped out of the deserted lot.

"Sally"—his voice was low and cautious—"Sally, I know how worried you must be, but Lou is going to be fine. The doctor said it was a minor fall."

"Don't. Don't talk about my father. Don't think about him. Don't be . . . anything *to* him."

The car raced through the twilight and on into the darkness, both of its occupants wrapped in isolating thought. It was a bruising, exhausting silence.

An hour later the lights of Kansas City flickered in the distance. Peter spoke.

"Sally, there's a lot going on inside that head of yours and I think we need to talk about it."

"And *why* do we need to talk about it?" Her voice was

as brittle as a dried branch, snapping off at the end of each word. "No. We don't need to talk."

Pete gently reached over and laid a hand on her shoulder. "Sally, I want to help. Don't you know how much I care?"

"No, Pete, don't! You must see. You're an intruder, a temporary diversion, nothing but a problem for me." He stared at her in disbelief, but she continued, merciless in her determination to have it all over, done with once and for all. "My life was clear-cut, tidy, before *you* barged into it." Her slender hand sliced the air in a staccato movement. "I was caring for my father in the best way I knew how, filling the void Matt left. I was giving Pop some joy and a reason to be proud. It was something to fill those long, lonely days."

"Sally, that's all well and good. It's noble. But what about *you?* You have a string tied from your heart to the past. Don't you see you have a responsibility to yourself as well. This is *your* life we're talking about. Yours . . . and mine too."

Sally felt his beloved warmth next to her. She could feel the familiar sensual stirrings that were never far away when she was near him. But she forced herself to push them away and braced herself. She heard herself lash out at the man who had fulfilled her in a way she had never dreamed possible.

"No! No! Stop talking about something that's totally impossible. We're fooling ourselves. This could never work for us. I have my responsibilities, my own goals and dreams, and they keep me here. And you, if it's not baseball season, it's training season, and half your life's spent on the road."

"That's just not true, Sally. Sure there's travel, time away. But there's time for home too . . . and a family . . . and love. Look at Joey and Gina. They've got some-

161

thing so special. There are so many others making it work, making it last. I'm not saying it would be easy or perfect."

"Perfect?" Her hands gripped the wheel until the skin was a transparent sheet over her white knuckles. Her heart beat wildly and her eyes stung as she forced back the welling tears gathered there. She pulled onto the road leading up to his house and sped past the gatehouse. "Perfect?" she echoed in a trembling voice. "You should have heard the wives at that party! They warned me . . ."

"And you'd let that count for more than what we have?" Suppressed fury shook his voice, and his anger shone dark in his eyes. "What we feel for each other? Here"—he pried one wrist from the wheel and pressed her hand flat against his warm chest—"feel that? That's me! A man. Real. Full of real feelings and passions. Not some possible problems and vague warnings."

"There's nothing vague about it, Pete!" Sally insisted, clinging forlornly to her decision.

"Okay. Then let *me* be perfectly clear! I think you're just scared, Sally Denning. Scared of having to change your mind, commit your heart. And I don't blame you, honey. I understand your feelings for your father, your job, your own dreams. I can share all that." He slid a finger across her wet cheek, trapping a teardrop. "Listen, I'm scared too. But, Sally, I won't let you build this wall between us to protect yourself. You don't need to do that. I won't hurt you."

"How kind and noble of you," she retorted.

"Nothing noble about it. It's pure, unadulterated self-interest. I think I'm crazy about you and I want you to stop being scared long enough to realize you're crazy about me too! And all these crazy, mixed-up emotions you're grappling with, well, there's always a solution."

Sally brought the car to a sudden halt outside Pete's house. A "solution"? How could there be a solution to the emotional chaos tearing her apart? Though her heart yearned to bend, her stubborn will held her rigid. How could they ever align his helter-skelter life-style and her clear-cut goals? No! He was fooling himself and trying to blind her too. She'd never fit into his life, and her own unhappiness and frustration would only make him miserable as well.

Overcome with sudden bone-aching weariness, Sally dropped her head onto her crossed arms on the steering wheel. She was just too tired, too utterly tired and despairing to try to explain any of it to him. Instead she turned and faced him. "I don't need solutions if I get rid of the problem."

Pete flinched as though she had struck him, but his voice was calm and deep. "Sally, you need to decide what you want."

Wearily, she shifted the car into reverse. And, tears streaming down her face, her voice leaden with despair, she gave him her answer. "I want you *out*. Out of my car, out of my job, out of my life."

CHAPTER NINE

Sally sat in the steamy interior of her little car, her legs sticking to the leather seats. The material of her skirt was limp and wrinkled already, her heart torn and bleeding. Her skin was damp, her mouth dry, she had stopped for a light just a block from WQEK and then, on impulse, had pulled into the parking lot of a 7-Eleven. That was where she sat now, staring blindly through the windshield. Even with the car top down there was no hint of a breeze. She pushed her hand through her hair, lifting the damp ends from her neck. She did not want to go to work today . . . could not bear to. Her spirit felt as wilted as her clothes. But what else was there to do?

With a sigh she edged back into traffic. The parking lot at work was full already. Others, too, had come early to seek refuge in the cool interior of the station. Grumpily she slammed the car door and got halfway across the lot before she realized she had left the keys in the ignition. As she reached in to retrieve them, her pocketbook bumped against the car door. The latch flew open and her wallet, checkbook, tissues, and melted Hershey bar all spilled out across the hot asphalt.

"Oh, damn," she muttered, tears of frustration springing to her eyes. "One more thing and it'll be the straw that breaks *this* camel's back!"

The climb up the front steps to the building seemed endless. The doors weighed a ton. The elevator never came. And when it did, it stopped twice before her floor. As the doors slid open, they framed two figures standing at the studio entrance. Robin, looking cool and fresh in a peach-colored sundress, was chatting away happily, her hand resting casually on P. J. Decker's arm. The two turned.

"Hi, Sally! What a scorcher, huh? It's the first time I have ever gotten to work before seven thirty. Beaver says he wants to borrow my sundress!"

Peter just looked at her, his face impassive. His brown eyes were dark, flat, obtuse. Watching, waiting. One dark wing of a brow lifted almost imperceptibly. His body shifted its stance slightly, one hip angling toward her.

Sally's stomach somersaulted in panic. "I forgot something," she mumbled, the blood rising to her ears and cheeks as she punched the first-floor button. The door clamped shut, blotting out Pete's bemused, offhanded grin, the maddening sureness of his glance, and Robin's open-mouthed look of surprise.

Once she was home again, she stripped, plunged into a cold shower, then called Bill Slater.

"Mr. Slater? It's Sally. I'm not going to be in today. As a matter of fact, I'm taking a week or two off. Yes, I *know* that's short notice, Bill, but I have the time coming, and—Wait, Bill, please let me finish. I was going to explain that Robin and I are already three shows ahead! There's nothing for you to worry about." She paused, listening, and her fingers tightened around the receiver. "That's nice of you, Mr. Slater, but, no, I'm fine. Just need some time off. Maybe it's the heat." She forced a laugh in response to his comment. "Yes, August in Kansas *is* a strange time to pick for a vacation, but I've lots to do and . . . well, listen, Bill, call me if you need me. Bye."

Sally spent the days inside, bathed in the artificial coolness of the air conditioner. There were things she *had* intended to do, things put aside and forgotten in the frenzy of these last months. She repainted her little kitchen, choosing a cool daffodil yellow that held the sunlight without its heat. She enjoyed the slap of the brush against the plaster, the long smooth strokes that hid what was beneath, the look of herself in the mirror—blond hair escaping from a scarf tied around her head, her nose and cheeks freckled with paint splatters. She read three Agatha Christie mysteries, sipping freshly squeezed lemonade through a straw as she lay curled on the sofa. She worked a needlepoint pillow she had intended as a Christmas present for Pop the previous year but had never gotten to. Well, it would be wrapped and ready for this year's holidays.

Early in the mornings, when there was still a light sprinkling of dew on the grass, she went for a two-mile run, waving to the other joggers, the dog-walkers, and the newspaper boys out in the coolness of dawn. At dusk she'd come to sit on the porch of the house, kept company by her neighbors, surrounded by their gossip and chatter, the click of ice cubes in tall glasses of tea, the familiar snap and hiss of beer cans being opened. She'd sit and read the evening paper, talk, and visit. It kept her thoughts occupied. Her mind focused on trivia.

One evening she was browsing through a trade journal for broadcasters and an ad caught her eye. An opening for a radio announcer in St. Louis. St. Louis! Two hundred and fifty miles away. Close enough to Dad, *far* enough from Kansas City. Quickly she ripped the page from the paper and headed inside, found paper and pen, and wrote a hurried but articulate letter stating her qualifications and asking for more information about the job.

That night she could hardly sleep. Her mind worked at

the idea like a dog at a bone. Here's the solution to all my problems, she assured herself. A new job, new challenge, new faces.

A familiar face rose before her mind's eye, imprinting itself on her eyelids. No, no. She tossed and turned, finally slipped from bed and made a list of all the reasons she should leave. It was a careful, logical list that demonstrated most definitely what a wise option this was. But a nagging, poignant ache kept her awake until morning.

The days passed while she waited for the reply from St. Louis. When it arrived she poured herself a glass of iced tea and sat in the sunlight at the kitchen table to read it. Yes, the job was still available. Yes, they were impressed with her credentials. Yes, they would like her to come for an interview the week of September 18. Over a month away? Her heart tightened with disappointment. Logically she had expected it, but emotionally she dreaded the delay.

It rained the following day, but in the late afternoon the sky cleared and a light breeze blew in from the north. That evening Sally took her newspaper and perched on the wide steps of the front porch. She was reading the comics when a shadow fell across her lap. Sally looked up to find Robin grinning down at her.

"Hi, Sal! I've missed you too much to stay away. Slater says hello—I think he was a bit concerned—and I've got hellos from Beaver and the whole film crew. And"—she lowered her voice—"from P. J."

Sally smiled. It didn't hurt *too* much to hear his name. "Oh, it's good to see you, Robin." She patted the porch step beside her.

Robin sat with her knees pulled up, her hands clasped behind her legs. "So, what have you been doing with yourself?"

"Painting, relaxing." Sally saw the deep concern in her friend's face. "I'm fine, Robin. Really! Don't worry."

"I can't help it. I never did understand what was going on between you and Decker, and then you disappeared."

"Nothing was going *on*, Robin. A bit of going around in circles, but that's all."

"You can't sell me on that, Sal. I know you better than that. And I've been watching Decker too. Oh, at first he was cool as a cucumber, but he's getting worried, Sal. I can tell."

"Robin, please. Let's talk about something else."

Robin eyed her for a moment, then nodded agreeably. "Okay, tell me when you're coming back."

"Monday, I guess. My vacation is about up, and—"

"Oh good, Sally. I have some good ideas for the show I want you to look at and, well, frankly I *do* miss having you around."

"Thanks." Sally smiled, a twinge of guilt stabbing her at the thought of her secret plans. "Thanks, Robin."

"It's not just me. Even Slater's grumbled about your absence. And now, with things up in the air again . . ."

"What?"

"Well, nothing is definite yet. But Decker is sure looking good. He complains that therapy is killing him, but he's looking and moving like the old P. J. I just wonder how much longer he'll be around. And I know Slater is hoping to get at least six more cooking shows taped before you head back to the sports scene."

Sally was awash with confusion. Here was what should be good news, but it felt terribly like bad news. She couldn't make sense of it all. To stop Robin's outpouring, she jumped to her feet and grabbed her friend's arm. "Come on, let me show you my kitchen. You'll love it!"

Monday morning, Sally pushed open the studio doors at exactly eight o'clock. A flurry of excitement greeted her arrival—smiles, a hug from Beaver, a wide, relieved grin from Bill Slater. Robin finally pulled her away and they headed for the cooking show set.

"All right, Sally, it's good to have you back. Now listen. I went ahead and chose six menus from the list you had compiled. And this morning we're going to rehearse the coq au vin show. I've got everything set up and the crew is scheduled for one o'clock for taping. So that gives us—"

"Hello, Sally."

"Hello, P. J." She felt the now-familiar weakness in her knees at the sight of him, but managed to keep her voice steady, her face calm.

"How are you?" he asked.

There was no denying how *he* was—darkly tanned, a pound or two in muscle added to his chest and shoulders, his brown eyes scanning her, cool and self-possessed. But there was the hint of tension in the fine lines about his eyes and a question forming on his lips.

"I'm fine, thanks. But I've got to run."

"Sally"—his eyes trapped her—"Sally . . . for god's sake," he whispered for her alone, "isn't it time you *stopped* running?" And he turned and walked away.

By Wednesday he had abandoned his attempts at conversation. The lines around his eyes were still there, but his lips were cold and set.

That was why Sally was so surprised to look up from her desk late Friday afternoon and find him standing there, watching her.

"Oh, Decker! You startled me." She laughed nervously before she could stop herself.

"Sorry." He moistened his lips with the tip of his tongue. "I've got something to tell you. I saw the team doctor yesterday and I'm back in the lineup. I'm leaving."

"Oh, Decker!" Sally leaped up, pushing the chair away with the backs of her calves. "Oh, good! I'm so glad! It's about time."

The hurt flashed bright in Peter's eyes. Jaw clenched, he

began to stalk away. Then he turned. "I knew you'd be glad. Got all your wishes, didn't you, Sally?"

In confusion she watched him walk off, arms stiff at his sides, shoulders squared. It wasn't until he rounded the corner that she realized he had misunderstood. He had taken her joy to be at his leaving, his absence, the return of her job. In truth, what she had felt in that unguarded moment was her joy at his well-being, his return to the life he loved. He had mistaken her love for spite. How could he? Her feet yearned to follow him, her arms to hold him, her heart to explain. But she restrained herself. No. Now it was over. Truly over. Leave it that way, Sally Denning.

That night she cried herself to sleep.

A pall lay over the studios on Monday and hung heavily throughout the week. Everyone from Williams to the office gofer missed P. J., missed his laughter, his warmth, his good humor, his sure courage. Sally tried endlessly to forget him, and was endlessly reminded.

"Hey, remember the time P. J. . . ."

"Look, there's the tape of P. J. and . . ."

"Gee, P. J. would have gotten a kick out of that . . ." It was anguish for Sally. The memory of Peter lay like the sediment in a glass of wine. Stir the wine ever so slightly, by word or thought or the mere mention of his name, and his memory rose up to fill her being once again. She circled September eighteenth on her calendar. The day and the possibility of a new job was the light at the end of a very dark tunnel.

That weekend she avoided Twin Elms. Sitting alone in her apartment, she read the Sunday paper, flipped half-heartedly to the magazine section. The full color front-page picture trembled in her fingers. Her heart twisted, and cold sweat dampened her back. Crumpling the paper, she tossed it in the trash and went outside for a run.

170

Next morning Robin dropped the same page faceup on Sally's desk. "Look at that, Sal! Look at our boy!"

There was P. J. Decker, flanked on either side by a luscious blonde, a broad grin decorating his face. And the caption: "Decker's Back—and He's Batting 1,000!"

Sally nodded curtly and pushed the paper aside. Feigning concentration, she stared stubbornly at the script on her desk. "I've seen it, thanks."

Robin gave her a long, knowing look and went away.

And then, that afternoon, the presents began to arrive. She came back from lunch to find a small box wrapped in flower-strewn paper sitting atop her desk. Sally looked questioningly around the room, but except for a shrug from Beaver she was answered with only curious, mildly interested glances. She lifted the edges of the paper, folding it back neatly in a habit left over from childhood. The snow-white box top lifted easily, and there, nestled in tissue, was a tiny enameled Battersea box, its hinged lid hand painted with the bright blue and white faces of tiny flowers—forget-me-nots. A dampness sprang to Sally's palms and she fumbled with the box lid, but Robin stopped her hand.

"Wait, Sally. Won't you show us what it is?"

Sally balanced the tiny enamel on the flat of her palm for the others to admire.

"Who is it from, Sally?" Robin was being painfully persistent.

"I really don't know."

"Here's the card, Sally," Beaver offered helpfully, but Sally caught the grin playing behind his beard. "I think it must have dropped when you opened the box."

Sally straightened her shoulders with a little jerk. "Yes, well . . ." She took the neat square envelope, slid it open, and withdrew the card. It had only his name—Peter.

She pushed the card back into the envelope and tossed it into the bottom of the box. "It's from Decker," she said,

171

her voice flat, her narrowed eyes forbidding comment. "It's to thank me for my help . . . and to say good-bye."

—"Uh-huh," Beaver grunted.

"What was that, Mr. Warren?"

"Nothing, Sal. Nothing." He was grinning broadly now.

"Better not be!" she said with the fiercest glance she could muster, dropped the enamel box back into the package, and slammed down the lid.

When the mail was picked up that afternoon, among the contents was a square package wrapped in brown paper, addressed in a stiff, angular hand to Mr. P. J. Decker.

Sally left the studio soon after, tossing behind her a curt "good night." Her little car echoed with her muttered curses. How dare he? How dare he play her for a fool in front of her friends! What was this, a joke? Or worse yet, a payoff? "For months of loyal service." She grasped the wheel so hard her knuckles were white. Did he think she was blind? Everyone had seen that picture plastered across the front page of the magazine. What was he trying to prove? That he was generous to the losers?

A restless night's sleep failed to refresh her.

On Tuesday morning there were a dozen deep crimson roses on her desk when she arrived for work. Sally dropped the card, unopened, into the trash, and marched the offending bouquet across to Robin's desk. Her scowl forbade even a thank you, much less a question. Beaver watched the proceedings with dark, sparkling eyes.

Wednesday Sally halted in the doorway before stepping into the office, her eyes darting around the interior, as if expecting a hiding enemy to leap out at her entrance. Beaver masked his grin with a wide, dramatic yawn, and the others kept their eyes carefully on their desks. It happened at lunch. Sally, Robin, and a young staff editor named Danny Gold were just heading out for lunch at a little Chinese restaurant around the corner, when the studio door banged open almost in their faces. A tall, swarthy man in a sparkling, spotless chef's hat and apron stepped inside. His voice rang like a bell through the small office.

"A Miss Sally Soufflé, please!" Sally took a half step backward, but her pride would not let her turn and run.

"I . . ." She dragged her voice from its hiding place deep in her throat. "I am Sally Denning."

"Well, then, madam. This is for you!" And with a flourish he placed an elegant carved silver serving tray on the nearest desk, whisked off the chaste silver cover, and revealed a still-steaming chocolate soufflé, its dark, puffed crust dusted with sugar, its rich, sweet odor filling the studio.

"No!" Sally gasped. "Oh, no! You take that back right now!"

"But, madam, my orders were to—"

"I'm giving the orders right now! You take that away."

"Oh, come on, Sal, be a sport," Beaver teased. "Besides, we're all starving for a taste."

"Then *you* eat it!" Sally sputtered, and with her heels drumming furiously along the hallway she disappeared.

By Thursday morning she had drawn one hundred deep breaths, counted to a thousand, and had fooled herself into thinking she was back in control. She stayed home until nine o'clock. Then with a firm hand she dialed St. Louis.

"Mr. Sandler, this is Sally Denning, calling from Lawrence. I wanted to check on the status of that job opening and tell you again how interested I am. Yes, well, I appreciate that. Is there any chance of moving the interview up to, say, this weekend? No, no problems here, I am only anxious to get the ball rolling." She listened to the distant response, then sighed, her shoulders sagging. "Certainly I understand—red tape and all. Yes, well, thank you and I'll see you on the eighteenth. Bye."

Later, in the office, Sally glanced up from the long computer printout of sports statistics that lay across her

173

desk and cleared her throat noisily. "All right, everyone, a brief announcement: Sally Denning would like to apologize for snapping your collective heads off yesterday. So sorry all."

"That's okay, Sal." Robin smiled, coming quickly to Sally's side. "But we wish you had stayed. That soufflé was yummy! And so sweet of Decker."

"Oh, yes. That's Decker all right," she mumbled.

The rest of the morning went smoothly. There were no surprises, no disturbances. Lunchtime came and went. The afternoon found Sally immersed in preparation for the evening sportscast. She and Jim Stafford reread the script, checked the teletype for the latest scores and previewed the film footage from last night's Royals game out in Oakland. Like a magnet the camera found Decker. Long and lean in the blue and white uniform, his body angled and ready behind third base. The camera zoomed in on his face and at that moment Peter looked toward the stands. Sally felt his eyes directly upon her, holding her, calling her. Those brown eyes with their hint of laughter and teasing. She flicked on the light.

"How about if you handle this footage tonight, Jim?"

"Sure enough," Jim answered, unaware of the tremor in her voice. "Funny, you know? He wasn't such a hot sportscaster. We're really much better, you and I."

"Oh, really, Jim?" Sally's loyalty flared. "And how do you think you'd do out on that ball field in front of thousands of people?"

"Hey, don't jump down *my* throat! I was just making conversation. Besides I thought you didn't care much for the guy."

"That has nothing to do with anything!" Sally felt the familiar tangle of emotions begin to well up within her. Hastily she began shuffling papers. "How about if we get back to these stats?"

"Fine with me."

After the broadcast Sally headed home. The evening was warm, the air was filled with the residue of the day's heat. Early September felt strangely like mid-August here in Kansas. But there was a lovely breeze that played among the color-tipped leaves of the old maples. The sky was just darkening as Sally turned the corner to her street. A small crowd was gathered in the twilight directly in front of her house.

"Here she is!" Mrs. McCuller called out. Her voice and the faces of her gathered neighbors were all colored with excitement. "Sally, come look!" cried another voice.

Sally felt her heart sinking like a stone into the churning pit of her stomach. Oh, no, please, not again! Warily she circled around the car, edging slowly toward the front lawn. The others plucked at her arms trying to hurry her.

A short, balding man in a delivery uniform pulled himself wearily from one of the porch chairs. "Sally Denning?"

"Yes, but—"

"Sign here."

"But what—"

"Look, lady," he complained. "I've been sitting here for over an hour. This is top priority, return receipt—first class. I was told to wait and I waited. But now I wanna get home to my hot dogs and beer." He thrust the clipboard toward her.

Sally locked her hands behind her back. "But I don't want it!"

"Lady, you don't even know what it is!"

"I don't *care* what it is!" she yelled back at him, her cool evaporating into the heated air. "I didn't order it and I don't want it. Take it back!"

"Sorry. I'm a delivery man, not a take-it-back man!"

"Okay, okay!" She grabbed the clipboard, snatched the pencil from its notched resting place, and stalked onto the front lawn. There, propped against the front porch, was

175

a gigantic rectangular crate. "Oh, lord." She halted dead in her tracks, astonished by its enormity. Then cautiously she paced in front of the box, carefully avoiding the dark shadow it cast on the green lawn, as though it held some trapped malignant spirit. Stamped across its front were assorted warnings: THIS SIDE UP FRAGILE HANDLE WITH CARE. And there, in the top-left-hand corner, was the stenciled return address: Sun 'n' Fun Hot Tubs and Whirlpools, 173 Main, Kansas City, Missouri.

With the sharp, slashing stab of a swordsman, Sally lurched forward, crossed out her name and address, and scrawled: P. J. Decker, Care of Kansas City Royals, Kansas City, Mo., across the front of the crate.

"There, sir! Now you can *re*deliver it! And good night." Without another word or glance, she climbed the front steps and let the door slam closed behind her.

Twin Elms. The sign hung above her, its painted green letters sparkling in the sunlight of another Indian summer day. As usual on a Sunday there was quite a bit of traffic heading for the home. Sally slowed and followed the car ahead of her toward the parking lot. She felt the betraying tingling of her frayed nerves—the too-rapid beat of her pulse. Today she was going to tell Dad about the new job. The interview last week had gone beautifully and the job was hers for the asking. Although she was here to ask Lou's opinion, her mind was really made up. She would still be close enough to visit and she'd make sure Pop understood that. There would be some changes, but she needed the distance, the time, and the chance to forget.

Red taillights flashed in front of her windshield and Sally pumped her own brakes. Something was wrong. The line of cars had come to a halt, and ahead and behind her horns began to honk. Impatiently Sally hit her horn. Then, with the unnatural restlessness that had possessed her for weeks now, she spun the wheel, pulled her little sports car out of line, and parked it at the far edge of the lawn. There! Let someone give me a ticket if he wants! She just couldn't sit still another second.

Dropping the keys into her purse, she headed off across the turf toward the main building. Something was definitely going on on this warm September day. Other people were leaving their cars now and stood crowded together in a wide half circle just ahead of her, blocking her view. She could hear young and old voices mingled together in laughter, a murmur of excitement carried on the breeze. She quickly searched for a place to step through to catch a glimpse of whatever was going on, and there, parked far to the right, previously hidden from view by the tangle of onlookers, was the Kansas City Royals' bus. Its exterior was painted with the team colors, and a vivid blue pennant bearing the familiar crown logo was draped along the near side.

Sally's heart thumped to a stop. Without a thought for appearances or politeness or courtesy, she shouldered her way through the crowd.

Stretched before her on the wide expanse of lawn was the clearly marked outline of a baseball diamond.

Sally stood with her mouth open, her eyes following the pattern from first base to second to third and home. Manning the field were some of the Kansas City Royals. Joey Rao stood poised atop the freshly rounded pitcher's mound, a switch from his usual catching duties. Owens and Dawe and the others were there, their faces creased in broad grins, their eyes twinkling.

At third base, crouched in the sunlight, was Decker. On the opposing team were the old folks, dressed in pullovers and faded slacks, cardigans and print skirts, each and every head shaded by a Royals cap. Wanda cheered hoarsely from first, one foot planted firmly on the base. Gustave was up at bat, elbows cocked, a wad of tobacco tucked in his cheek, his gray eyes and jutting chin mirror-

177

ing his delighted determination. Behind him, already shouldering a bat, stood Lou Denning. The gray hollows of his cheeks seemed filled out today, and his skin had the ruddy glow of pleasurable exertion. The thin strands of his gray hair stuck helter-skelter to his forehead, but his eyes were sharp and bright and clear. Past the field, lining the wide front porch, Sally could see wheelchairs and walkers, backed by the nurses in their crisp, starched uniforms. The patients were busy clapping and waving their canes, cheering the team on.

"Go get 'em, Gus! Make it a home run!"

Sally stepped forward, drawn by the sights and sounds and by the nearness of the man she had tried so hopelessly to banish from her thoughts.

Lou caught sight of her. "Hey, Sally! Hi, honey. Come give your old pops a hand here. This team could use a good pitcher!"

Decker turned. His eyes found her face. Held her. That crooked smile that broke her heart washed over her in welcome.

A matching smile found its way unbidden to Sally's lips. Her eyes misted with tears. Tears of love and gratitude. Peter had somehow coaxed and coerced his teammates to take a Sunday afternoon away from the grit and glory of the pennant race, a precious Sunday without a scheduled game, to bring life and joy to these old folks. These elderly men and women who still held the boys and girls they once were locked somewhere within them. She saw that youth and shining brightness sparkling through their eyes now. The years fell away as bent backs seemed straighter, knotted bodies seemed smooth and supple. He had worked a miracle. He had stopped the hands of time for one brief, eternal moment, and they would be able to look back on it later and find the strength they'd need on quieter, lonelier days.

His dark eyes still resting on Sally, Peter touched two

fingers to the brim of his cap in salute and reluctantly turned back to the game.

Gus hit a base hit and sent Wanda storming to third. The crowd went wild.

"Atta girl, Wanda! Show 'em your colors!"

"Give me a *W!* Give me an *A!*" chanted those on the porch.

Lou was up at bat. Knees bent, his bat resting on his thin shoulder, his cap pulled way down over his brow, he peered fiercely from beneath its brim. "Come on, Rao, let 'er rip! Come on, young fella, watch what a little experience can do!"

"You tell 'em, Lou!" Pete yelled, straightening from his ready stance to grin in encouragement from across the field.

Wanda stole home.

"Hurray, Wanda!" Sally flung wide her arms in delight, at the same time casting away the cares and confusion that had confined her spirit. "Come on, Pops, show 'em what a Denning can do!" Sally cheered, hopping from one foot to the other in excitement. The tall fellow to her right plucked the blue Royals cap off his own head and tugged it down over her shining blond hair. Sally's eyes danced and she nodded a thank you, then took a step toward the base line. Leaning forward, hands on her knees, she shouted across the field, "Come on, Gus. You can steal third, right out from under Decker. Just keep your eye on the ball!"

Pete tossed her a teasing grin over his shoulder. "Hey, no coaching from the sidelines, even from gorgeous blondes!"

The game rolled on through the early afternoon sunlight, and when the ninth inning ended, the Twin Elms Twisters emerged victorious, the score three to two.

The crowd swept the players up into the welcome cool of the front porch. They gulped glasses of Gatorade, munched platters of lemon cookies. Patients, visitors, and nurses clustered closely around Pete and the other Royals, collecting autographs, signed baseballs, and kisses on wrinkled brows. There was much talk and laughter, but time and again Pete's eyes sought Sally's face. She knew he was looking for her and struggled to get close, but the press of humanity held them apart. She had to talk to him, yet she didn't know what she would say. More than the words, though, she yearned for the touch of his hand, the heat of his body.

The crowd stirred, shifted, and for a moment Sally thought she saw her chance, but once again he was swept away. Those who could were forming two long lines, standing shoulder to shoulder behind the long chrome row of wheelchairs. Sally felt a stranger's hand around her waist as she became a part of the living chain, and together they sang "Take Me out to the Ball Game." The husky voices of the players supported the tenuous voices of the elderly.

As the song faded, the deep bass voice of Walt Gregg, the third-base coach, rumbled over the crowd. "Okay, boys. We've got that three-o'clock meeting. Better get rolling or we'll be up to our necks in hot water!"

The crowd surged toward the waiting bus. The players were surrounded by the waving, cheering throng. Sally dropped back forlornly, sure that Peter was about to be whisked away without her being able to speak to him. Her heart was breaking. Then suddenly his tall, lean figure broke away from the group. Eyes riveted to hers, he maneuvered his way toward her, brushing past the restraining hands, ignoring Gregg's warning voice.

Before Sally could sort out her emotions, he was at her side, his hands warm and strong on her narrow shoulders.

"Sally, I have to talk to you."

"Peter—I know. There's so much to say, so much . . ."

180

"Listen to me, Sally. I know you're confused. I know you doubt me and the life I live. You sent all my presents back."

"Oh, Peter, let me explain."

"I can't now. There's no time and I don't know if you should have to."

"But I think I want to."

"Sally"—he bent his head and his lips brushed against hers—"it's time to decide *what* you want."

Then he was on the bus. The door snapped shut and he was gone.

CHAPTER TEN

Sally gunned the engine in the already agitated little car and begged it to hurry. Come on, baby, she crooned to the inanimate vehicle, get in gear. Please, don't fail me today! The battered little car answered its owner's urgent plea and lurched forward, then steadied out to a smooth cruise and took off down the highway.

Sally held a shaking hand to her breast, then breathed a sigh of relief. The coveted press pass was tucked into the pocket of her soft burgundy blouse, its stiffness forming a rectangle in the silky material. Car, ticket, now, if my nerve and patience will only hold out until I reach the stadium. Please God, she prayed silently.

She switched on the car radio to steady herself and hummed along with the soft, soothing music for a moment, then lapsed into thought.

"You're a Denning. Don't ever forget that. A Denning plays clean and from the heart." Lou Denning's voice was strong and clear in her ears.

After the wonderful baseball game with Peter and his friends, she had found her father to be more lucid and alert than he had been in months. And in the course of their long father-daughter talk, Lou Denning had emerged strong and in command. He had opened Sally's mind . . . and freed her heart.

"I love you, Sally dear, always have. It's *you*, not your damn job and your career aspirations! You, the joy of my life." He touched her cheek and there was a glistening in his crinkled eyes when he added, "You've done a damn good job of growing up, Sally. How did an old codger like me raise such a beautiful woman?"

She could still feel his kiss on her forehead, and his familiar chant, straight out of her childhood, echoed even now in the small, speeding car: "We're Dennings, right? We're fighters, right? Take it. Run with it. And fight for it!"

Right! The answer leaped from her heart. It was all suddenly so clear, so obvious. All her life she had been a fighter. Even as a child, she had hidden her tears, girded her spirit, and sought her goal. She was not going to look back on that with regret now. No, she was proud of who she was. She liked Sally Denning! And if she had made some wrong choices, at least they had been hers.

But she was *not* going to make a wrong choice now! Her future lay within her, unformed, like a budding flower. The fear of relinquishing her own childhood passions and the uncertainty of the present moment were there. She knew she had been using her father and the memory of Matt and her job as a shield to protect her from Peter Decker and the changes and choices that loving him would bring. But in a moment of wondrous release and resolve, she faced the reality that she did love this man with her whole heart. She would surrender all, risk all.

A weak laugh escaped her lips as she remembered that she had never even mentioned the St. Louis job to her father. She never would. The only future her clear hazel eyes could see centered around a laughing fair-haired man in a baseball uniform.

"Come on, you old heap!" Sally crooned, her blood pumping through her veins. The girl looking back at her in the rearview mirrow had wind-tossed golden hair, bright points of color high on her cheekbones, and love-filled eyes.

Sally spun the radio dial, seeking something special, and stopped when a baseball announcer's voice filled the car with excited pregame patter.

The whole town of Kansas City was wild with the hope of pushing their team on to the ultimate baseball glory. Kansas City had World Series fever! The airwaves, the newspapers, the streets themselves were ablaze with this all-consuming excitement. Peter had fit back into the team as if he had never been away. He was batting .350 and throwing balls as well as the team's best. But in Lawrence, Kansas, just fifty miles down the interstate, Sally felt a million miles away.

She had tried to reach Pete at the team's office, the stadium, his home.

"It's time to decide what you want, Sally," he had said. Now she knew. I want you, Peter Decker! But she could not find him to tell him. His housekeeper, Ella, had been the only friendly voice she could reach. Pete was staying in town, she had told Sally, and there wasn't any sure way of reaching him before the playoffs began. The team, especially Pete, was using every moment to get themselves ready for the opening game. But keep trying, Ella had encouraged her. Keep trying, Sally dear. If it's important, keep trying.

So keep trying she did. But after more futile attempts to reach Peter by phone, Sally planned a new, more daring course of action. First she cautiously approached Bill Slater, then pleaded with Harry Williams, but it wasn't until she approached the grande dame of WQEK, Adelle Williams herself, that her plan began to take form and life. A hopeless romantic, Adelle had hung on every word of

Sally's story and at the end had not only come up with the press pass for the opening day of the playoffs, but had offered, an offer Sally graciously declined, to accompany her to the stadium.

"Oh, Peter," she murmured aloud as she pulled the car into the tangled streams of traffic stretching toward the stadium. "Oh, please be glad to see me. Please, dear. I don't know what I'll do if you're not."

The press pass got her through the booths at the entrance to the parking lot. Had *everyone* decided to come early today? she fumed, unable to stem her growing anxiety as she joined the long caravan edging along onto Stadium Drive. She flashed the pass at the attendant and was waved into the small lot reserved for the media. Her hand tightened around the rolled banner that lay on the seat next to her, and clutching that in one hand and her precious pass with the other, she raced to the stadium. The steep three-story escalator seemed suddenly too slow for her anxious feet, and she took to the ramps, flashing her pass at the indignant guards. Up in the press box she slid through the covey of reporters pressed against the railing and peered down.

The Royals were on the field as she had expected, it was too late to catch Pete in the clubhouse. Now she zeroed in on him. His image filled her horizon . . . and her soul. Gone was the ease and lightheartedness that had graced him. He was coiled tight as a spring. His jaw was a flat, hard line, cut in granite. His arm was tense, the fingers gripping the ball fiercely before he leveled it to Rao. The others were a blur, a shimmering blue and white kaleidoscope of moving and shifting patterns across the field. Sally saw only him clearly. She ventured a tentative wave, her elbow held close to her side, her fingers waggling. He never looked up. Growing more bold—more desperate perhaps—she reached out over the rail and waved broadly. Still he didn't look. Then, as at a distant trumpet call, the team turned and left the field. Sally, watching the figures disappear into the dugout, leaned even farther, lifting her knee onto the top rail for a final try.

"Cut that out, lady! Who are you anyway?" Two firm hands gripped her waist.

"What? Oh, sorry. I forgot where I was."

"I bet! You looked like one of those 'flies' they catch trying to go over the rail to kiss one of the players."

Sally blushed furiously, her tongue trapped at the roof of her mouth in embarrassment.

"Hey," the same voice, edged with contempt, drawled on. "Who were you eyeing anyway? Decker, I bet! Now that he's back the women are all breathin' heavy again and lining up at his bedroom door. I also bet"—Sally felt strange fingers locked about her wrist—"I bet that's not even a valid press pass!"

This threat to her hard-won press seat brought back her voice. "It most certainly is, sir, and I resent your accusations! I am Sally Denning from WQEK." And she turned her back, tossed her hair, and stormed to her seat.

Moments later the crowd rose to its feet as the players returned to the field. The opposing teams formed two nervous, shifting, tobacco-chewing, narrow-eyed lines. The scheduled celebrity stepped from the courtesy car onto the field and filled the silent stadium with the sweet, heart-piercing strains of "The Star-Spangled Banner." The last note died on the air. There was a moment of pure silence as the crowd, like a wave gathering force to itself for the crest, took a deep breath, then roared its approval and encouragement for its beloved boys in blue.

Sally cheered as heartily as any of them. When the Royal pitcher struck out the first three opposing batters, Sally leaped to her feet, her cheers joining the echoing storm of exultation that swirled through the stadium.

Dawe had a base hit, a young rookie named Wyckoff

doubled, and the next batter brought them both in. The Royals were on the scoreboard.

The next inning was slow, a duel between the two pitchers as each fought to keep the other team from scoring. Sally's attention drifted from the field back to the dugout. There was no glimpse of Pete. All that was visible was a row of caps and uniformed shoulders lining the bench, the players looking like parachutists in the belly of a plane, masked with the same heightened but grim determination.

The third inning brought the opposing team to the scoreboard. But the pitcher held them to a single run. Then the Royals were up again—Owens at bat, and Peter stepping from the shadows of the dugout into the golden gleam of the sunlight. The crowd went wild, shouting his name, chanting it with the fierce adulation that only true fans can understand. Pete reluctantly stepped farther out onto the field. He nodded once, raising his hands to quiet the fans. They screamed even louder. And in the seconds that it took for the noise to ease, Sally could see P. J. Decker as they saw him—the Golden Boy, the hero. At the same time, through eyes of love, she saw the Peter only she knew—the farseeing, self-knowing eyes that swept the crowd, the smile that acknowledged its love but knew its fickle nature, and accepted that ungrudgingly, the set of the broad shoulders that spoke of strength in a gentle man.

Her heart bursting with love, Sally was on her feet again, waving with the blind hope that he'd see her, but knowing he wouldn't. The same reporter cast her another derisive glance. Sally merely tipped her nose heavenward and sat back primly on the edge of her seat. She was up again when Owens singled. And remained there, mesmerized, when Pete came up to bat. They walked him, throwing wide around him. Afraid of him, Sally knew proudly. The next three Royals were struck out, falling like dominoes in a line, and the inning was over.

Sally ate her way through the next inning and the one

after that. Her nervousness held her in its shaking grip. It was either a hot dog drenched in mustard, or all the nails on her right hand. The hot dog won, and then a malt, a stale pretzel, a platter of nachos. The others began to stare at her incredulously, nodding their heads in her direction and eyeing her over their ever-present notepads and pencils, their sleek black cameras.

Sally ignored them. She was past noticing anything. Only Peter and her own body, aching with unspoken love, were real. Only them. Alone in the world. Then Peter was up at bat again and her emotion overrode her restraint, her body was two steps ahead of her mind and she was at the rail, leaning precariously across the top rung, leaning out over that emerald field, out into blue space . . . looking down with love at that beloved face and form.

"Peter! Pete Decker, look up! Look up, Decker!"

And he did, shading his strong tanned face with the flat of one hand against the sunlight's glare. His deep dark eyes melted into warm cocoa as he found her. He stood still, staring up at her, while a murmur of sound rippled across the stadium.

"What's going on? What's happening?"

"Wait, Peter—Wait a minute!" she begged him. Tearing herself away from the rail, she turned back to her chair and grabbed the rolled banner lying there.

He hadn't moved. The waves of sound were growing louder, more insistent. But the two of them never heard. Sally smiled once, a loving smile that drifted down to him on the sunlight and touched his face and lit it with answering love. Then she tugged off the ribbon that held the banner and flung it open across the rail. It read, simply, for all to see: I LOVE YOU, PETER DECKER.

He stared, first at the banner, then at Sally. A titter of incredulous laughter rose from the stands. They had seen it all before, these Royals fans, and they were not going to be surprised by just another woman, albeit a very attractive one, making a fool of herself over their charming third base man. What *did* surprise them was P. J. Decker's reaction. He ignored their laughter, his fine, handsome face turned up toward this presumptuous flaxen-haired girl. With great seriousness—a quiet, restrained passion that glowed about him like a flame—he touched his hand to his heart, then to his lips. He loved her. He had all this time, she now knew. And he would truly, for all time, she was sure.

The crowd was hushed as he walked back to the plate, swung his bat to the ready angle above his shoulder, and nodded at the pitcher, who wound up and threw the ball. With a crack that echoed through the still-silent stadium the ball reversed direction and flew like a winged wish over the outfield wall. Home run! The crowd was in ecstasy, cheering the long, lean figure who rounded the bases and trotted home.

Again Peter sought only Sally's face. He smiled, a swift, leaping smile that lit his dark face with unexpected sweetness. A timeless moment passed between them. He touched two fingers to his cap and stepped back into the dugout.

The Royals caught fire after that and swept the rest of the game out from under their opponents' feet. Then it was over. The first game of the playoffs was theirs. The fans swarmed over the rails and out onto the field, mobbing the players in wild celebration, even as the guards herded them toward the gate.

Sally had fled in the opposite direction, down the curving ramps, out through the side entrance, and around to the locker room door. It opened even as she approached. Peter stepped out, his uniform clinging to his sweat-drenched body, his face flushed with excitement.

"Sally, my love." He caught her in his arms and held her pressed against him as though afraid she'd vanish. "Sally? Did you mean it?"

189

"Oh, yes, Pete, yes." She stood on tiptoe, her arms wrapped around his neck. "Yes, I mean it, my love. You are all that I want . . . and all that I want is you . . . I love you so!"

He cupped her face in his broad hands, tilting her chin until he could search her eyes with his own. "No restraints, no restrictions, my Sally soufflé? No more presents returned unopened?"

"Never," she whispered.

"But you know what waits for us. The crowds, the fans, the crazy schedules, the weeks on the road. I can't make those things go away."

"You don't need to, darling. It's you I love. All of you, who you are, what you do. And I love you so much that I won't be afraid to share you with all that, knowing your heart is mine."

"Heart and soul, Sally. For always." He bent closer, his dark eyes sparkling. "And your job?"

"Don't worry," she said, snuggling against his chest. "I promise to be totally unbiased in my coverage. Besides, I cover best on the bias, if you know what I mean."

"I can't wait to find out!" He laughed softly. "Marry me, Sally."

"Does that mean I get an exclusive on you, Mr. Decker?" she teased, her eyes filled with love and consent.

"That, and a whole lot more." And his strong arms wrapped about her in a promise of forever.

Candlelight Ecstasy Romances